Sergeant Getúlio

João Ubaldo Ribeiro

Houghton Mifflin Company

Boston 1978

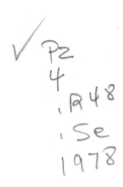

Library of Congress Cataloging in Publication Data

Ribeiro, João Ubaldo, date
    Sergeant Getúlio.

    Translation of Sargento Getúlio.
    I. Title.
PZ4.R48Se 1978   [PQ9698.28.I165]   869'.3 77–10799
ISBN 0–395–25705–0

Printed in the United States of America

v 10 9 8 7 6 5 4 3 2 1

To Rona

In this story Sergeant Getúlio takes a prisoner from Paulo Afonso to Barra dos Coqueiros. It is a tale of virtue.

Introduction

Among the works of fiction published in Brazil in the last decade, few have been as important as João Ubaldo Ribeiro's *Sergeant Getúlio* for the development of our fiction.

The importance of this novel is, among other things, that it makes possible the harmonious development of the literary art by preserving and deepening the most significant traits of a literature characterized throughout its history by its persistent concern with exposing both individual and social problems; in other words, a literature free of all gratuitousness.

Another reason for the novel's importance is the language of *Sergeant Getúlio,* the fruit of a literary idiom which has been taking shape for a long time, based upon creative work with the vital, popular, rich and free language that is Brazilian Portuguese, so distant from the Portuguese of Portugal in spite of their common roots.

In recent years, perhaps because of the political situation experienced by our country, the affirmation of Brazilian literature in the novels of the thirties has been counteracted by a process of alienation from our own values, a process that can be felt not only in the field of literature, but in every area of artistic creation. Such is the case, for instance, of Brazilian popular music, which is every day less popular and less Brazilian.

In conjunction with this abandonment of Brazilian sources of artistic creation, there is an elitism of expression, artificial and elaborate, which completes the dissociation between works of art, particularly literature, and the people from whom they arose and for whom they should be destined.

It is significant to notice that so-called committed writers, engaged in dealing with social and political problems, are not immune to this process. On the contrary, in the works of many of them this alienation and this elitism are immediately and deeply felt. An odd contradiction results: Works that aim at being innovative, even revolutionary, in their commitment to faster social change are read and understood only by an ever smaller group of initiates, so they lose the capacity to reach the class of readers who are really interested in deep social changes.

The purely formal experiments dominant in the work of these young writers have led to a literary language unrelated to the language actually spoken and continually enriched by the people. The lack of originality in these formal "researches," which alter so much the character of our literary language, and the preoccupation of these writers with fads and faddisms make their works empty and foreign to our people.

Born in the state of Bahia, on the island of Itaparica, and spending much of his childhood in the neighboring state of Sergipe, which for various reasons is a different country with a face of its own, João Ubaldo Ribeiro first emerged as a writer in an anthology that gathered together four talented young short-story writers. Soon afterward he wrote a novel,

x *Setembro Não Tem Sentido (September Has No Meaning);* but publication was delayed so long that when the book finally appeared the author felt himself to be distant from his text. That does not detract from the interest of this first novel, a restless narration about young intellectuals in search of their own truths in a still-provincial city, as Bahia was in the author's youth. The book earned a *succès d'estime* and the critics took notice of the young writer. Soon thereafter they felt the impact of *Sergeant Getúlio,* so different from what is in fashion, what people wish to impose artificially, what deserves only the most facile applause.

Sergeant Getúlio is a novel that not only avoids the alienation process, but also points to the way in which Brazilian literature should evolve, experimenting and innovating. In developing an extremely rich narrative voice, the novelist makes use of his deep knowledge of the language spoken by the people, of the most profound reality of our people, and so his literary language is a fertile and powerful instrument of creation, competent and faithful in its artistic representation of the life of the Brazilian man. It is the opposite of the empty and badly contrived language of the elitism mentioned above.

The language in *Sergeant Getúlio,* artistically molded on the speech of the people, is often terse, hard, and cruel, rejecting all the usual mannerisms, the easy artificial games played by falsely modern writers, which are nothing but sad academicism. And this language gives very proper expression to the strong substance of the book, which is treated with extraordinary ability in original technical solutions. Among the mass of books published in Brazil in the last ten years, *Sergeant Getúlio* stands out as one of the few works contributing to the development of a literary art that is genuinely Brazilian.

João Ubaldo Ribeiro has not stopped at *Sergeant Getúlio.* Since this great novel he has gone on to write a book of short novels, completely different but of the same high quality, and he continues to write about the people of Itaparica, Bahia, and Sergipe, the common men and women, the animals and trees, and all things large and small, for there is nothing in his rich universe to which he is indifferent.

Jorge Amado

Salvador, Bahia, Brazil
September 1977

Sergeant Getúlio

I

The great pox is like this, it's always on the move. If you leave it alone it shrinks you up and turns itself into all kinds of other distempers, so that one should always guard against women on the road. First rule. From Paulo Afonso to there, a long stretch, especially by night under these conditions. An oxcart road, dammit. There are all those villages and towns out there, Canindé de São Francisco and Monte Alegre de Sergipe and Nossa Senhora das Dores and Siriri and Capela and other such scattered places, God knows how many. Propriá and Maruim, you know what they're like, dust and cotton bales up on the trucks and the raw dryness out there. And rough country, cactus and catchweed, everything sting-ing, thorns underfoot, a nightmare. The plants and the women equally disease-bearing, you could get skin sores from them, all kinds of treacherous creatures, ticks, scor-pions, chiggers, think of it. Back there I killed three wretched characters on top of some low thornbushes; one of them fell to the ground slowly, worrying about the thorns, no doubt. Now there's a question, whether someone who is about to die worries about comfort? If I were a knifeman I would have finished him with the steel blade, but it makes a strange sound and is untidy because of all the blood that comes spurting out. And so I shot him in the back of the head from a special position I know that doesn't waste ammunition. And I called him names on top of that for making me go hunting in these badlands, running around in this white heat and hashing up my brand-new field boots in these knotted vines. Nothing to see but melon cactus and brown bushes and rough grass and buzzards. He didn't even hear me, he just folded up and went cold. A routine job. How far would he have made me go? Itapicuru? Vitória da Conquista? I don't know. There are no limits to the weakness that makes a man bolt, turning his soul loose in the world, running from his destiny. A man's hour is a man's hour. That bastard lay there, sprawled flat in the thorns as though the ground were covered with floss. What difference does it make? Whoever has seen the final shot knows how it is. That jerking in the body, a shuddering once and for all. Then it's the buzzard's turn, since the job is no longer one of punishment, but of cleaning up. The buzzard is the broom of the desert, he notices the minute somebody stops walking in these backlands and he wheels overhead like a spirit. He wheels like that, snapping his beak and oof-oofing his wings, making those ghostlike hops and sprints, cursed ghostlike. He goes and goes again, comes and goes. In mourning. He must have remarkable breath. It is known that the buzzard is born white and then he turns black and if he sees a live man he gets sick to his stomach. They make us sick, we make them sick. Out in these backlands, when all the potholes run dry and the birds are grubbing the mud on the riverbed, there is a large silence. Only twigs crackle now and then. Just like swamp trees, only this is not a swamp. There isn't a man born who does not fear the buzzard, because hunger makes him bold and he hops closer to you, little short hops and leaps, his

2

wings wide open and his great beak wheezing. He's the master of the world. You can see his tongue and you can hear his steps in that little round walk of his. You can expect that the man will be eaten pinch by pinch, by jerks. The creature stretches backward, drags his catch across the dirt and swallows it, tilting back his head, and all this in great silence and dispatch. The second unfortunate was liquidated almost the same way, only he was more resigned, he was saying his prayers. They say he had been bitten by a barber beetle, he would have died of blood disease sooner or later anyway, but he seemed sound and healthy to me. Anyhow, whoever eats a piece of jack fruit and drinks any kind of hard liquor on top of it, his skin breaks out all over, but in the hours before that happens everything looks excellent, until the breaking out begins. So they say; I've never seen it myself. I was never a man to let a Christian mix unmixables in front of me, such as drinking water after chewing sugar cane, or eating coconuts when you have a cough.

A natural death leads to ugliness and bad feelings because it moves slowly, it is not peaceful. I always say at street celebrations, when people gather together like natural fools prancing back and forth, I always say, look at God's chickens. Just like a regular back yard chicken. When it least expects it, while it's just chickening around the yard, just picking and pecking around with that stupid chicken face, the owner catches it, shaves its neck very carefully and bleeds it into a deep dish with a little vinegar in the bottom. When we least expect it, God catches one of us and twists his neck and it's no use crying for quarter. Same thing. Appeals to Saint Lazarus, Saint Cyprian, are of no use, because saints have no prevalence over fate. The creature melts down to his elements. National Democrats, Social Democrats, anyone. Amaro's seen many a bastard in his agony, haven't you Amaro? He won't talk when he's driving, nothing you can

3

do about that. Except when he gives some whore a ride. Now, we're not whores, at least I'm not a whore, excuse me. Hey Amaro, uh-huh Amaro, hey you blight, when a man talks you answer. One of these days with these bad manners some man is going to rip you apart and all you'll have time for will be to glance at your bowels, pray half a prayer to Our Lady and pick the best spot in the dirt to lie down and do it fast because maybe before you reach the ground you'll be dead. How about that, Amaro, considering you're so lily-livered. You know this pest here is from Muribeca. The people of Muribeca are good for nothing, they're all hicks, there's nothing there, you know. Amaro, either you speak up or I'll take offense. Right. Ho-hum. Tush-tush. This road is an oxcart track, everything falling apart. I've chased a lot of men down roads like this. For minor cases, you devise remedies in accordance. We have two large casks at the Frei Paulo police station that are supposed to be filled with water. When we catch the man we make him bring water in two leaking kerosene cans to fill up the casks and he has to run, otherwise the water will run out before he gets to the casks, because there are many holes in the cans and we studied their placement with care. Manioc pies for food, if anything, stale or not, depending. They sour in a man's stomach, they can give you the heaves. Sundays there are beans with one or two kale leaves floating in that brownish water, not very appetizing, it's not my problem. More serious cases require the flushing out of the so-and-so. Half a pound of uncooked salt codfish when you can find it, and if you can't find it use cheap jerked beef instead, just like it comes from the general store, no cooking, no boiling. Next a glass of castor oil, the fat kind that makes bubbles that pop open and smell of fresh castor beans. Listen good, creature: If you let your insides pour out in this county, we'll be having a bad feud, and you'll lose. You think he doubts it? He whisks himself away

4

even on horseback if he can find himself a horse, or then he scampers on foot and goes to relieve himself beyond the border. From Barracão to Simão Dias, I don't know. I won't allow that sloshy crap where I have my jurisdiction. Never. I did things like this several times, so as not to do worse things. A fellow like that may have a wife and children, he squeaks like a butchered hog, what are you going to do? A need is a need, as long as my horse and I are all right I don't give a damn, as they say. A campaign worker of this kind deserves no respect. Even now that I've lost some authority I still have my influence. I have good backing in the capital city of Aracaju and my name isn't Getúlio if I'm to give up all of a sudden. Especially after delivering you. There is some good feeling for you in Aracaju, people in your favor. One of those things. I don't like this assignment, I don't like to escort prisoners. It puts you out of face. After I take you there I'll set up my quarters somewhere and give up this footloose life. I won't change my mind except if boss Zé Antunes insists a lot. Even if he insists. I'm retiring. This bottled water is warm but it's good. Never drink water where you can't see the jug. Second rule. Lampião used to carry a silver spoon in his saddlebag. And he would stick that spoon in all his food. If the spoon turned dark it meant the food was poisoned, inasmuch as poison darkens silver, as you know. Certain death for the man of the house. If the spoon didn't become black he took to giving presents and stocking up stores and sowing happiness in general. Often he would lose his temper over some little thing. He used to put a man's nuts in a drawer, lock it, throw the key out and set fire to the house. Not without first leaving a knife within reach of the wretch. The way I see it, it's better to burn to death than to lose your nuts. Your voice gets thinner and thinner and so does your beard, you become pederastic, false to your body. But most people prefer to cut their balls off rather than turn into charcoal. Nowadays that kind of thing isn't done anymore. Would you put up with a thing like that? There was another time, when Lampião tied up a judge's wife, maybe it was in Divina Pastora or Rosário do Catete or Capela, he tied this wife of this judge to a tree and stripped her stark naked. Now whoever saw an old woman like that with so much hair on her parts? Have you ever seen such indecency? Not even the worst whores, how about that? And he peered over his glasses this way and that way, and ended up pulling all the hairs off the woman's twat in front of everybody, everyone gathered there on Lampião's orders, because everything he did was always in front of everybody. There was great badness in him, he killed without ideas. So naturally he ended up with his head cut off in Bahia and put on exhibition like it was a wild bull's horns. But before that he played hide-and-seek with every state militia that was after him and he left his mark in the world ever since the time of the emperor. So they say; I never saw it myself.

Hey Amaro, where do we happen to be? Let me know when we get to Curituba Velha, I fear ambushes. The worst thing about this heat is the little bugs that come flying through the window and stick to the sweat on your face. Pestilential family of animals. In Buquim, all those mosquitoes, you should see them. Is Buquim Brazil? Porto da Folha is Brazil, with all those blond people drawling. Aracaju is not Brazil. Socorro is not Brazil, is it? Bahia is not Brazil. Bahians sing when they talk. Necessary to take a bath one of these hours. Goddamned heat. And these bugs hitting a Christian's face. I'll retire. A house in Japaratuba, which is a quiet and cool place next to the Japaratuba River, of which the only defect is that it starts over in those boondocks of Muribeca, eh Amaro? And then I'll just stay there, eating crabs. Write my name on the ears of two nanny goats and just stay there playing backgammon. Milk pudding, how about that? A calm life, you know? And I a man who has killed twenty people. More than twenty. You wouldn't know it to look at me. But if I weren't alert I'd still be back there in the nameless backlands chewing wild beans, thin as a son of a devil, a couple of scraps for possessions, a heap of children, a pinch of food every week and a wretched nag to round up strays for some rancher. Waiting for Saint Joseph's Day, those heartless droughts, hopelessness. That rain, that before it gets to the ground rebounds on the heat and steams back up, the godforsaken land so scorched it's like flames. Japaratuba is less savage. I'll buy binoculars with the intention of looking over the land. I like binoculars. Over twenty people to my credit, imagine, it's like women, impossible to remember them all. The first one is the most difficult, but after that you learn not to look at the face so as not to bungle the job. When you're too close it's no good. They grab at you, they pull your jacket down. It's true I'm not in uniform most of the time, but when I am I get angry when my uniform is messed up. I don't like to wear an incomplete uniform. Rotten little road. I don't know, maybe it would be better to buy a good farm, a quiet piece of land. Manioc. Funny, it's poisonous but I never saw anybody die of manioc poisoning, though everybody knows it's poisonous. Killing with poison is dirty. I knew a corporal who drank ant poison and vomited all over himself. An ugly death, purple vomit all over the bed. The third one who died in the wastelands, I don't remember his name. He had a face like a disturbed turkey's, a red face. His was a slow death. He was a tough one, he defended himself with a machete, so we had to fill him up quickly with lead. Even so, Alípio's cheeks got a horrible cut and flapped right open like two leaves. A bad wound. I have to buy some pomade for my hair as soon as we get to a town that's fit to live in. When I'm in plain clothes I don't have my cap to hold down my thatch. Alípio wanted to talk but he 7 couldn't, he could only blow without checking his wind. From which it is evident that the place of speech is also in the cheeks. Not much blood, just enough to smear his neck, more or less. His cheeks like two flags, one rubbing against the other. I'll buy a nice-smelling pomade and have my sideburns trimmed. Alípio pricked the National Democrat's guts with the bayonet three or four times. Most National Democrats take a long time to die, they hang in the air like a chameleon. Except for the women, who die like anybody, National Democrat, Social Democrat, Labor, Fascist or Communist. Don't know much about women, anyway. The great pox, the smallpox plague. The great pox will make you crooked like a hook. Some people take women's medicines to cleanse their body. I don't know. It stings. Even at night this dust gets in and dirties my shirt, all yellow. Amaro likes to speed down the road, but on a cartroad like this you can't do any better.

I'm sure you're not in a hurry, you. I'm going to buy Oriental Petroleum Hair Lotion, just like the boss does and goes out sticky and smelly, strolling down João Pessoa Street, white-suited and with a handkerchief in his pocket and making his usual stops to talk and explain things and then sitting down for a beer, and cheese with black sauce. My opinion is that the boss mounts the women of all those insignificants whenever he feels like it. A woman goes into that office room and she comes out heavy. That's my opinion. Oriental Petroleum Hair Lotion. Dammit. Cursed flies. Flies don't drown. As a boy I used to catch flies and put them in a bottle of water, and then I shook it well and when I opened the bottle out comes the fly like nothing has happened. It resists well. What annoys me is that you shoo it away and it comes back to the very same place where it was before. Of course you can catch it, if you put your hand a handspan and a half away from it and sweep your hand more or less upward, so you grab it in midflight. Then if you throw it hard against the wall it gets flattened. But I can't do that here, there's no room. Oriental Petroleum Hair Lotion — have you ever used it? If I had my hair straightened maybe I would look better, but if I wanted to have it straightened I would have to go to a beauty parlor in Aracaju. Impossible, I would end up making a couple of holes in some people, if they looked at me funny. Aracaju is more difficult than the other towns, a big city has too many witnesses. Politics are no good in Aracaju. If you want a man's politics, look for it here. Hell, there are even rove beetles in here, have you noticed? Those bastards make water on your face and it gets all lumpy, it never heals. Amaro, we'll sleep in the first place we come to, I can't stand this trip anymore. Hell, even rove beetles. When I was a boy, I used to get red bugs from lying on the grass. It's necessary to smear your body with sulfur powder and water and to bake in the sun until the pests relent. It stinks like the devil and I used to get all scaly and yellow. They're bad bugs, those red bugs. Watch out when you lie down in any bed, stay always alert. Third rule. A lot of good men died for sleeping unarmed. I have to buy a radio. It's fashionable. The man I killed in his bed, I killed his whole family. Mysterious massacre in Itabaianinha. A massacred family. And by then everybody's making fools of themselves and I'm sleeping in Arauá. I don't like newspapers like you do, I find them difficult, too many words. Lies. National Democrats, Communists. Communist National Democrats. Social Democratic party. When we went to pick up this fellow at the whorehouse, he was all dolled up in a linen suit and shiny tie and laughing like he was in a big party. Tárcio pushed the door open and let out that big holler. Did you know the late Tárcio? Amaro did, hey Amaro. Did you? Ahn. Hum. He let out that yell he was known for. I'll round up all the men and geld them! One side, one side, one side, and   9 come through this door to be searched. The place crawled with whores, all of them dashing through doors, slipping under the beds and everywhere else. They gouged one by the back yard wall when she tried to jump out. I forgot to say the back yard was surrounded, we even had men on the roof, and all of them very bad men. And in the middle of all this confusion the man wanted to make a speech. What is the meaning of this? What is the meaning of this? What is the meaning of this, Sergeant? I am sorry, senhor, you are going with us, your honor. The woman who owned the house started talking with a Rio accent, pretending she was worth something. Tárcio grabbed her by the head and threw her inside. You think she ever shut her mouth? She went on saturating a man's patience, so Tárcio went over and popped open his blind eye on her and huffed on her: Stop annoying us, loose woman! Who ever saw a whore with rights, wherever? When the devil can't come, he sends his secretary. This Rio slut, accustomed to having everyone drooling over her ass. Out, out! Get back, you bitch! And she backed down and held her tongue and Tárcio popped open his blind eye on her one more time and the whore quieted down.

That milky eye of Tárcio's killed many people of heart attacks. When he became annoyed red veins appeared too, it was awesome. The boss said: Bring this man alive, Sr. Getúlio. I want him here, alive and kicking. The man was brave, he wanted a fight, but his shoulder holster got stuck and the gun didn't come out and so it was his end. A barrel hit across the face — he squirmed a little here and there, and stopped. He went very, very tamely, his lips broken open. Tárcio wanted to give his hair a close shave, but it was not possible. It was just a matter of giving him a few instructional blows, it was not like the day we busted the Communist newspaper. No one ordered this busting, but that paper annoyed the boss, so one day it was burned down and there was no water for the firemen. There was nothing left of it, and there was a Communist crying by the door. A very yellow individual. From Bahia, no doubt. Thin and meatless, he must have been weeping like that out of weakness. In any case, burned is burned, and nothing survived, not even a burning splinter to light my cigarette. It was the end of the National Democratic Communists. Those Communists are a chickenhearted lot, although they are fond of disturbances. When things get tough they vanish in the air. I got a lot of them. Luiz Carlos Preste, Luiz Carlos Preste. They had concentrations at the Plaza Pinheiro Machado shouting that, and once they blocked all of Frente Street, they wouldn't let anyone pass. We wouldn't listen to any excuses. "My friend Getúlio, understand this well: Use your club on this rabble." There they were, carrying on like monarchs, and we thundered out of the Plaza Fausto Cardoso and started breaking heads. A company of dogs, don't you agree? Not a head remained unbroken when the mounted police trotted up to the square. As for the newspaper, afterward the boss announced in the other newspaper that it had been burned by the Fascists. "Get those Fascists, Sr. Getúlio, so they will learn not to burn other people's newspapers. Bring me all of them, for the love of God." We went to get them and pretty soon we had more Fascists in front of us than we had use for. A pretty thing to do, to set fire to the Communist newspaper. As they went into the station they complained and complained, "But it was not I who set fire to the newspaper, But you can't do that, But the man's father is important and will get him out" and things like that. They marched in anyway, an inquest was opened. As far as I'm concerned, they may all still be there.

These people are no good. They went to the boss's place and gave word that — an informer warned him — they gave him word that they were going to get him at home, and if   11 he wasn't home when they went for him they would get his wife, and if she wasn't home they would get his son. Reinforcements arrived from Bahia, they put dogs in the yard, we hid the boy and deployed ourselves under the trees of the plaza, all over the gazebo and the gravel. It was war. Tárcio and I stayed in the porch holding two well-oiled machines, two brand-new machines. To enter was to get filled with holes. And we were ready to sweep that square with a lead broom, a festival, huh Amaro? When there was silence you could almost hear the guns breathing and feel a heavy air, the Virgin Mary help me. Amaro saw it, hey, he was wetting his pants there, packing a short-barreled gun. Hey Amaro, can a gun fire without a man to pull the trigger? If you're born in Muribeca, are you a Muribecan? Ha-ha. A Muribecard or a Muribecian? What a character, Amaro. A good chauffeur up there, a steady hand. It is he who drives the boss's Studebaker in times of great need. He and Batista, but I don't like Batista, do you know him? Well, there we were with our elbows on the sill, wondering whether the invasion was coming and being careful to keep our heads inside, for it was quite possible that they might send a slug from Cedro Street and we are not birds to be shot at just like that. Tárcio went out from time to time, his head turned up because of the blind eye, to pick up a piece of salami at Zé Corda's store, sometimes tapioca cookies which he enjoyed, a bottle of soda pop, things like that. Not me. I stood fast. As for the National Democrats, they were as present at the place as you were. They knew the Social Democrats were ready for just any kind of politics, no matter what kind. And that was in Aracaju, because if it had been in the interior we would have done to them what they did in Ribeirópolis, as a matter of fact I know you took part in that, when they set fire even to live cattle and spread salt on the land and pulled doors and windows off the houses of our people and put a man outside every one of the holes that remained, so that they could keep looking in. This they don't remember or talk about. But that day they did not appear, it was the highest kind of politics, inflamed and violent, it was going to be a slaughter. We had hands good and willing, a circle of lead. But they didn't appear. If they had, it would have rained iron. Cristiano Machado is our man, Cristiano Machado. Brazilian. A President is a President. A National Democrat is a National Democrat. Maybe I would do better, instead of Oriental Petroleum, to get Glostora Pomade, because I like the smell better. You remember that black called Ramálio, Amaro? I'll tell you something, that one was a thief, he was good for nothing, he got what he deserved. They tied him behind a car and dragged him around. They threw the remains in the swamp. A bad black, from Bahia. To be both black and from Bahia never comes out well. Well, he used Glostora, that miserable character, see how he had nerve. I am going to have these sideburns trimmed. A real man was President Froriano. That's what they say, I never saw him myself. I don't know how old he is. Every Peixoto is a man. The old people know that.

But have you ever felt such goddamned, mind-boiling, stupefying heat? Do you feel that? What feels good is morning by the mountains, when the mist hasn't lifted yet and that wispy smoke comes out of your mouth when you speak. Or else the sugar cane plantations, hey Amaro, the sugar cane fields in Riachuelo, looking in some respects like the sea in Aracaju. It's a shore and sea of sugar cane, you have to see it, the reeds bent by the breeze. This you feel from up on the hills because from lower down it looks like upside-down brooms, little brooms, and each one like a blond head. It's best in the morning, when the woods are still quiet, without the bugs and the game birds swarming around. I have a sister who didn't find a husband and now lives by the window   13 with the other spinsters over in Vila Nova and she enjoyed looking at sugar cane fields in blossom. She was the one who taught me to like it too, because at first I didn't notice it, it went unappreciated. Now I like it, and when the time is right and I have the time I spend a long, long time looking at it. Good coffee, cigarettes and a lot of peace, almost too lazy even to lie in a hammock, enjoying all things. One can think about life as if he didn't have a thing to worry about. But that's all, because soon the sun gets warm and as it gets warmer the woods come alive with animals and it all itches and makes life uncomfortable. Plague, there is no place to live. A sugar mill is good, because no one can pull a man out of one of them. I don't really like that, you know. No one is allowed to enter a sugar mill to haul a man out. I don't like that, it's against the law. It ought to be against the law. Why does a man have the right to spend his life as a runaway, sitting tight in a sugar mill? It's privileged. But now just as I was thinking about life, the bread of Inhambupe came to my mind. The bread of Inhambupe is exceptional. Have you ever eaten it? Amaro has. Haven't you? Hum. Shoo. What a bread. Inhambupe is in Bahia but it's not in Bahia. When we get to a town, I'll also give my boots a shine. Right after I arrived in Aracaju, before joining the force, I used to be a shoeshine. I was just a little boy, with no worries in life. Fighting just for fun, silly little fights. Although you can kill with a slingshot too, come to think of it. That's what they say, I've never seen it myself. Only pigeons. Maybe I should see a doctor, I've been feeling some pangs in my chest. I can't understand how a man can spend his life feeling other people's parts. A profession is a profession. I don't like doctors. I never shot a doctor. Or did I? I can't remember. They say Sinimbu was a doctor in Pernambuco. Now he's deceased, and that's it, he's not a doctor, either in Pernambuco or in Petrolina. Nor in Maranhão, nor anyplace, not even Judas's ass. Greasy bastard. They gave him a bath and rubbed him with corncobs, they really rubbed, although it never became red where they rubbed, since a dead body won't redden, it just lies there motionless and getting stiffer. Nobody minds if the dead person is dirty, just put his voting clothes on him, stick him in the coffin, and that's finished. Gravedigging, what a miserable profession. All men from Paraíba are grave-diggers. Paraíba is Brazil. Damn this lousy dust, it can give a man a cold. What a disgrace, if you blow your nose you get some kind of clay. The thing to do is to have some tar brandy.

See now, what an idea, to bring you from Paulo Afonso, right within the state of Bahia, up to these lost lands, a short trip so far, if it wasn't for this blessed shit of a cartroad. I'm already filthy and with mud running down my neck. Imagine the late Cavalcanti, whom they brought from Paulo Afonso in an ambulance that was more like a bus than an ambulance, with twenty-six slugs in his body in several positions, and that beast was still alive in Aracaju burping blood, and they had to drain blood from a good number of people to put into him. Twenty-six holes in that frame and the beast pushing death back with great courage, like a fighting rooster. I don't think you have ever seen a man resisting death, because what they tell me is that you give orders, you don't do things yourself. It's all right in your position. But see here, when a man fights death back there is no more horrible apparition. When assistance arrives on time and reaches him while he's still alive, you can see his chest going up and down and those gasps of agony and that uneasiness and that struggle and the head turning and the hands clenched. If you've never seen it, you don't know what it is. There are people who say death comes softly. There are those who say it even gives peace, like when you're starting to rest. That may be afterward, because when the time comes the sufferer opens his eyes   15 wide and holds on to whatever he can find, as if he were holding on to life. And he turns around and gnashes his teeth and raises his head and pulls in the air and tries to talk and peers about and goes mad because everybody else isn't going with him and makes his lips purple and makes as if he's going to sit up and rubs against everything and drools and shakes on the sides and glares at people and belches and shivers all over and feels sorry for himself and stretches his legs and makes scared faces and twitches and makes noises and farts and wets himself and cries and thinks about whatever he never did and begs for the Lord's mercy and kicks the wind and pulls on his clothing and swells his chest and in the end he makes an effort and turns his eyeballs in an awesome way and pulls up all of a sudden and goes his way, because the day comes to each and every one of us. A man's time is a man's time. But nobody likes to go, that's priest talk. There is no danger on this earth that some man hasn't seen to tell how it is. But when you meet death you can't tell about it later, it's final. Who wants to be put to the sword? You may have seen riot-control cavalry in action when sabers are permitted, for hitting the flat sides against the mob. Spirited, fiery horses, hoofs in the air. Neighing heavily. And hoofs on all sides, everybody getting their equal share. Once in Buquim we set up an ambush on horseback. First you catch the last one, like you do with game birds. The first one you catch with the second volley. Being a man who doesn't like showy weapons, I took my Smith along, but Tonico took the dwarf machine gun, and he used it and it wasn't a nice thing, because men's brains and jaw splinters were flying everywhere and there were pieces of people all over, just like when they killed a certain somebody in Itabaiana Grande. The orders that came were, don't touch the body. But there was hardly any body at all, when that gun spurts it sprays blood in all directions and leaves nothing in one piece. Tonico enjoyed it, he was more of a gunfighter than a politician. I'm political, I don't kill for nothing. Tonico laughs when he shoots, he's not decent, which is the reason why over a hundred people took the oath of death on him. He is known as Jaguar Hand because his hand doesn't shake when he's using the old stutterer, he only wrinkles his forehead and bites his lip and holds tight. He points it ahead like this and holds down all that jolting steadily, even though the thing pulls left all the time, exploding one firecracker after the other. This time it was in Salgado, and the investigators came from the capital looking like a procession, with everybody talking in whispers and wearing heavy coats. It was very chilly and there were a lot of people out in the street for that hour of the night. I was still there, dressed in my black overcoat, when the men arrived and I popped up in front of them. Here I am, Senhor. The doctor told me, have a man collect the body, Sergeant. He didn't even know there were two bodies, not just one body. Oh well, you couldn't really tell, with everything jumbled up in that mess, a real soup. I ordered two men to gather the pieces but they didn't do a perfect job, because some ants scurried up to the place and carried away the smaller pieces, and the rest of the pile was crawling with them. The doctor said, "How come you didn't mind the bodies, Sergeant, and let the ants carry away the pieces. This is disgraceful and speaks badly of us." And why this and that, it's not right, you hear? Because this speaks badly of us, you hear? And I replied, standing at attention: "But, your excellency, either I did something about the ants or shot the armadillos, you know armadillos are crazy about corpses. And there were a couple of six-banded armadillos around there, scampering about as is their custom. It would have been worse if the armadillos ate them." And I actually had hit an armadillo, which lay there much more in one piece than the two men, since it was I who shot it, not Jaguar Hand   17

Tonico. He had cleared out a long time before that. The boss came, the funeral was well attended, and we had armadillo stew. "Senhor Getúlio, there will be no one left alive in Sergipe if you go on like this, we can't do that." "Dirty National Democrat," I said, and spat out the chewing I had in my mouth. The boss let out one of those hollow horselaughs, his eyes on the ground and his shoe tip scratching the dirt. That day I gave him a blackbird which I blinded myself, and he would have it to this day if he hadn't given it to a friend who calls on him now and then and whom I don't like. He has a face like an opossum's. He's a born witness, worthless. Cursed road, I thought the time had passed when I took truckload after truckload of voters to the polls around these parts, you see. Once some people tried to steal a truckload of voters from me at gunpoint and it was quite a shootout. We lost two votes in the brawl, but they lost more, and those were votes already counted and paid for. A tough people. Sergipe is one big backland, even if it isn't.

You excuse me, senhor, but keep away from that door. As a matter of fact, that's the one that was shot by machine gun, so it won't open no matter what you try. But don't lean on it just in case, because I have responsibilities concerning you. Forgive me for talking all the time. It's to keep from sleeping. I don't even know when I'm talking and when I'm thinking, I can't tell very well. You don't have to answer, although it represents a lack of education. It's like so: If I sleep you will do what you can to take away my gun, hit me, shoot Amaro in the back of the head and slip away through the scrublands until you find shelter. Meanwhile, here I am chatting as if you were my bosom friend and we were baptizing one of our sons. Oh well, I can't say you enjoy talking to me, because I know that if I dozed off you would pull my faithful six-shooter off me and drive a bullet through my temples. As for 18 myself, if I woke up in time to catch you pulling out my gun

I would drill your skull with the very same gun, and I couldn't care less if you told me you had been to high school. Remember: If instead of picking you up in Paulo Afonso with all possible care to bring you on this goddamned, merciless trip, dammit, dammit, dammit! shit, Amaro, hold down this fucking Hudson, this son of a bitch is falling to pieces! If instead of bringing you with me I had put you to the steel and stuck your head in a straw bag there would be a great many happy people in all of the state of Sergipe, you shithead, I don't mind saying it, shit, shit, you shithead, heart of turd, son of pestilence! Look at this trash, get a load of him, Amaro! running away to Paulo Afonso, why, running away to Paulo Afonso, running away to Paulo Afonso like a stray cow, you pile of filth! running away to Paulo Afonso, to Paulo Afonso. I would follow you to hell, you hear, you stinking dog of stench, I'll finish you, you shameless queer, spineless fairy, filthy cocksucking pantywaist of the devil of the pox of the basket of manure, prick lover, you went to high school, you went to high school! a high school never made a man out of a bum, and don't answer because it's better for you, I'll stick your head in a straw bag and leave the rest to the wild dogs, you filthy mutt, you think you're something special, now answer me, you crooked-tailed capon, trash! slimy capon, I might just pull out one of your balls this minute to see you down and one-balled in Ribeiró-polis in a couple of minutes, runaway slave, son of a mare, son of a cow, son of a jackass, yellow skunk, bastard, bastard, bastard, bastard! I'll eat your soul, I'm not joking! I'll slice out your liver, I'm not joking. Why, running away to Paulo Afonso, shacked up with a whore, what more, senhor? Now, think about it, Amaro, I tell you. Stay out of this, Amaro, when a man's head heats up better let it cool off by itself.

Did you ever go to high school, Amaro? From what I've heard, you used to wash the stairs of the State High School.

If washing the stairs of the State High School gives a man learning, you're doing well. Ask this Communist here, this dungy queer, this bad pox! Ask him but don't think he will answer, because he will not. He talks only to educated people, but there he is with his lip flicking like a newt's tail, afraid I will put an end to him right now. And I will, trash! Oh well. Shoo! Ahn! Shrivel up, you bad sort, shrink yourself right there, that's your place. Keep off that door, you prick face! Off! Should I give this bastard a little pounding, Amaro? I guarantee that when he pulled the trigger to butcher a whole family, he wasn't even thinking about it. He was as brave as a man can be, all jaunty, all courageous, just like one of Lampião's henchmen, oh you nameless pimp, you cheap gunman. Now tell me. If you piss in your pants I'll cut off your rod and dump cement on the stump, I'm warning you. You're lucky that they want a trial, there are newspapermen in your favor, a whole system of people. If I had my way, everything would be done quickly, with your head in the straw bag to be delivered neat and trim, with hairpins. But if you get less than thirty years, no one will escape, neither you nor the prosecutor, the judge, the lawyers, whatever. And if you get more than thirty, you will die anyway, when you come out. Your life makes a turn, and in the end it comes and goes to the same place. Amaro, we will sleep anyplace where there's a house nearby. Help me tie this thing to a tree. We're not going to untie him for his needs.

II

I live everywhere. I live walking. Ay, aaaaaaaaay, aay, aay, ay, ay, aaaaaaaaay, aaaay, ay, a clay bull, ay a clay bull, a clay bull, ay a clay bull, alas, a clay bull, ay a clay bull. I live walking, like this. A cattle chant, said to me. Said to me said to me. Ay, a clay bull. Have you seen those little bulls of all colors, especially the color of plain clay? I am now covered with clay like this and I eat of the clay as though it were food, because of the brown taste. As a little boy, in the market, let me tell you. When I arrived it was not yet broad daylight. Two, three windows, maybe four windows, were hung with salted meat in large and crisp strips, black or white, according to the fat in them. Memories of food feasts, and the smell. Sometimes a funeral in the early morning. Had to be early, because one needed to work. A dead person doesn't eat, so perhaps it's better that way. But being early didn't make it less of a funeral, rather it made it more of a funeral, because at other hours there are people in the streets not paying attention to the funeral. Not so in the early morning because when there's a funeral at dawn the funeral is the only thing there is, with that coffin slithering by and the people behind and you can hear footsteps and trouser legs rubbing against one another. Also water jugs at the windows, sweating. I used to like to rub my hand on the bellies of the jugs, to slap the sieves hanging from the roof, to look at rocks. Some of them cracked. Whenever I could, I used to crouch in the shade and make a powder out of the ones that broke. It was a good powder, you could mix it. Sometimes we challenged each other about who had more powder, who had more different kinds, who had the finest one. Sometimes a whole day like that, boys are silly. My powder is more, your powder is less, I have blue, I don't have blue. There were stones that changed color. We used to keep the powders in boxes. But we always lost them; no one keeps powder very long, not even a boy, because it was of no use but to see colors anyway, and there was very little time for such things. Sometimes little time, sometimes a lot of time. Sometimes quite a lot of time, as when it looked like rain but it wasn't rain, over the canvas of the stalls. It became dark and the clay bulls stopped in their rows. Because if you looked at them in the sun, you would see them move in those long, long rows, so long that in the end they came together. And the heaps poised one on top of the other, on top of the next, on top of the next, like this. So that in the sun they all glittered and flickered like thundersparks. It was a motion we knew wasn't there, but it was, and the boys would stare at the bulls, thinking of herds and roping calves. In the rain there was nothing, only puddles. But before the rain it stopped. Everything stopped. I used to sit on a tree stump, musing. Everything still but the thoughts. Speech was still. If your vision traveled from one end of the street to the other, it could only go slowly because even your head seemed to be under water, a thick air, a soft and still thing. Nothing with the bulls, they were all frozen. I say that time dismounted and there was time for everything, because life didn't move. But so much time meant no time at all, for there was nothing to do in those hours.

And the city called Orange Tree seems to be dying anyhow, like the stone dogs balanced on the columns of the big grilled houses. I never saw so many grilles as I saw in Orange Tree, I might say that. I mean, yes I did, but there seem to be more grilles in Orange Tree. I don't know how to put it. There are more, and there is a flatness to the ground, so that it helps you to keep a steady mind holding your eyes fixed to the ground, choosing your steps and walking firmly, so that you forget about the scenery, but when you raise your eyes there it is, the same great grilles, so many grilles, most of them brown, some of them sharp-tipped, some round-tipped, only the grilles and some old girls with their elbows screwed to the windows, gazing about deathlike, all wilted, they don't even speak. Once in a while one of them turns her head around and stays like that a long time, head turned and no will to turn back around, so she stays there like a plant. They don't even have anything to talk about anymore. You can't hear a thing, all you do is look at the grilles. In Orange Tree the world is grilled. It is a grilled and straight life and all of a sudden, when you least expect it, the street ends and nothing follows, or then the same thing starts all over again like a wheel, the same grilles and worn-out walls. And the whores, I didn't even know what they were, waking up with their hair standing on end and their red eyes peeping out of the houses. Now I understand, it's the life of a whore. Sluts, wenches and harlots who help us in our suffering like the cows of our Brazil. Every day Orange Tree dies a little more. One day it's going to die all the way and it'll stay among the grilles like a dry cashew and those who pass by will say, there is a dry cashew, and they'll keep going on their way. In the backlands there are no grilles, and there are not many other things either. There is more land, anyone can see that. 23

I think there are more goats. Sometimes I'm at peace like I am now, just brooding over things in my mind, and I remember something that must have happened long ago and it seems to be happening now. I'm talking or doing some little thing such as picking up my tobacco with my left hand or putting my hand in my pocket or looking at somebody's face or asking what time it is, I'm just sitting there when it comes to me that this has already happened sometime. I mean, not really the same thing, but something like it, almost the same thing, and it's as if I knew what comes next, but I soon forget about it and I return. It's just one moment, but it comes like a funny feeling in the belly. I did this once just like now, I once did the same thing. Right here. I consider this for some reason I don't understand. As I sit here, this Orange Tree thing comes to my mind. If it was the backlands, it would be easier to understand. When you're lost in these wilds, you get to thinking you're back home. But not Orange Tree and those grilles. I don't know the reason. It might be because it's going to rain, maybe, and the weight of the weather brings me ideas. I won't untie him from there, not even if it rains. I don't like him. He can catch cold, he can catch anything he likes, I don't think he's going to live very long anyway. He's a bad man. First: He gave Ocridolino poison in the hospital, when Ocridolino was about to leave, and killed him on the spot. Second: He had Anfrísio shot as he sat in a wicker chair by his door, wearing his pajamas. Third: He dried up Ribeirópolis, he challenged the Paraíbas. He sowed the land with salt, threw out their belongings and killed their calves.

I haven't forgotten to this day the time I drove into town with the car's siren wailing. I used to press my knee against the button and it went off like a thick, long meow, and we went on stirring up dust with that meow in front of us. There was a Social Democrat banquet, they foretold deaths and everybody had their shoulder holsters on and there were

24

guns everywhere, like in an army camp. We sneaked along the alleys, Tárcio and I, and it was a nice walk in the shade, with the wind funneled our way, so that's where we stayed. The rest of the men were deployed around the house and the corners of the banquet house's porch. It was a force of wicked men as no one had ever gathered together. Let me tell you, if there had been any combat only the wind would be left there, and a stinking wind at that. I stepped out of the car for a while, I could feel the smell of bad men in the air, the walls seemed to be alive with eyes. Tárcio said, tipping his cap, go but don't expect to get back, and if you get back you'll be full of holes, he said, looking like he was talking about soccer or going out for a bite to eat, looking like nothing at all was going on. If I could miss a man, I would be missing him. He shook my hand when he died, but he didn't die that day in Ribeirópolis, it was later, in Riachão do Dantas, and he died with his bowels showing. But I went anyway, I strutted down there, they had paper pennants hanging from the wires and colored lights, and all this of a very cheap kind, such as you would expect from a place like Ribeirópolis. It was hot out in the main street, because there wasn't a single tree for relief and the sun hurt my eyes when it rebounded on the white dust that covered the ground. So I went strutting down the street, tipping my cap with my thumb and hearing my boots creaking in the silence over the fine dust. I wanted to get something to drink, but I soon regretted the decision, because the blessed dust was flying up to my groin, I could feel it, and my boots getting dirty and spoiling my elegance. Everything was completely motionless; it seemed that that cheap population was afraid to take a stand, you would think they were unaccustomed to politics. I felt like talking out loud to myself, hey won't this stupid mayor ever pave this street, senhor, and what a cheap, trashy city this is, senhor, look what a disgrace, senhor, and   25 things of the sort. But when you're on a mission you can't go around making trouble, so that I went on lifting one foot carefully behind the other, so as not to mess up my boots so much, one foot behind the other, one foot behind the other, and Tárcio's face in my memory. I knew he was pretending he was asleep in the car but he was more awake than a rock lizard, that good-for-nothing, he closed his eyes with his hand resting on his instrument, he was no fool and anyone could test that who dared to. A white dust like I never saw, so fine and like armpit powder, very fine dust. I kept walking and stepped up to a sidewalk three handspans high and stomped on the curb to shake the dust off my boots, ahn, the pestilence won't fall off. The one at the counter glanced at me like he was afraid I was going to shoot him, but I said nothing, I only closed my fist and stretched out the little finger and the forefinger, and said, one. He poured two in one, he looked like a rat. And I stayed there a while, watching the snooker game they were playing, thinking that as soon as the festivities started across the street all these people would be wiped out, but then no one moved when they destroyed the houses of the Paraíbas and did all those rotten things. They didn't leave a single door or window, even your needs had to be taken care of out in front of everybody. So I stayed on and on, I even whistled, knowing they were more scared of me than of the devil, and I stayed on and on, sometimes looking at my nails, sometimes scratching my balls, sometimes pushing and pulling the door back and forth, just for presence. Whenever it came to my mind, I glared at one of them, but they turned away. So I wiped the counter with a handkerchief, planted my elbow on it and stayed some more. The banquet was probably at its height by now, so I decided to go back down that disgrace of a street again. I do believe that if I had ordered it, they would have picked me up and carried me so I wouldn't have had to put my feet on the ground. All I had to do would be to say, I don't like the ground here and if I have to set my foot on it I will become angry. But I didn't say anything, and went back to lie down in the shade inside the vehicle and listen to Tárcio's stories. Tárcio could make up verses when he wanted to, and he could also memorize them. I memorize very little, being a man of little learning, but if I had more learning I would memorize more verses, because I enjoy them and everybody enjoys them, and when a man is not doing business but doing friendship, when it's the early evening or the early morning, and you can talk without thinking about what you will say, you can make a verse, you can have peace, you can linger with your thoughts, feeling the hour, feeling that very hour.

> My dear friend Getúlio
> Allow me to tell you
> A story that once happened
> In the village of Propriá.
> There was so much death
> Even the devil went there.
>
> Women turned into men
> And men turned into women
> And even the wild beasts
> Ran as they saw what happened.
> Only a man of great faith
> Will believe in all of this.
>
> The river was split in the middle
> And the woods were opened wide
> Just like in Saint Noah's time
> When the world came to an end.
> And all this was on account
> Of a man who came to town.

This man answered to the name
Of Such-and-such Honorato,
Born of a heathen woman
And of a shameless father,
Raised on wildcat's milk
And of very bad manners.

When he slept he was bad
Even worse when awake.
He killed four people a day
And said, Are there more?
And one day just to round up
He even killed his grandmother.

The day he came to town
And what a town it was
There was no government left
And also no police force.
The mayor dirtied himself
And the officers were scared.

He knew them all and he said them slowly, keeping time
with a finger going up and down. If it weren't for his being
a man, I would miss him. Sometimes he laughed and slapped
his hands on his legs, raising his body in the chair. But he
didn't laugh much, because he was always frowning and
looking off into the distance with that one eye. He could
have died in Ribeirópolis, except that nothing happened that
day, since the cowardice of the National Democrats pre-
vented the festivities from starting. But when they felt like
wrongdoing they went right ahead with it, and that which
has no remedy can be considered remedied. There is no
honor on the way out. You're out, you're out, and that's it.

So I can't stand this one here. He's no good. You can't tell
by looking at his face. You can never tell by looking at a face,

I know that well enough. I've known that since I was a boy, you can make many mistakes. Now he's over there, tied to the hog plum tree. I'm not going to untie him even if it rains, and I wish it would, so I could go near him for a closer look, and say a couple of things to him, make a little fun of the bastard. Taking a little shower now, one can see you are a gentleman, with your officer's haircut, a very clean man with slanted sideburns who chooses this hour for a cool shower. We're having a little rain, huh? I could tell him, it's no use having other party members, no use, go fetch your fellow party members. Just call one and see, come on. Ahn. Politics is a man's business, I could tell him, if he got scared as I assume he would. I would like to say that, I would enjoy it if he got scared and whined like a woman in labor, if he squirmed and did all kinds of things. I get angry inside, it seems I have a need to be angry. Besides, another one or two will make no difference, it happens all the time. You start dying when you're born. Tárcio used to say, I only dig the holes, God is the one who does the killing. The same thing, even Tárcio himself, who came in with both hands folded on his saddle pommel and full of holes, I'll never forget. If he could die, anyone can die. So. Death may come quickly. It's a relief. This vale of tears, this crap. Dead bodies are like wild squash in this land. They cover the ground. Heh. Cover the ground. Shoo, I can't even tell you. I myself am standing here like a pole but can tip over anytime. I arrive — hello, how is everybody, a very good afternoon to you — and then it's time to go — good-by, a pleasure to see you people. Who cares. We're all alone.

I used to think differently at times. She was with young at the time. I used to stroke the belly when I had time or when I felt a quietness coming or when it was warm or when I lay down or when it was misty or when it was peaceful. She was like a dog, she sat there with her clear eyes gazing at me.   29

The round belly brought me satisfaction, you could guess well what was in there and the bellybutton stuck out a little bit, I could feel it with my hand. So I kept stroking and stroking like in a daze, thinking about the little creature inside. When I killed, I wasn't even thinking about killing any longer. I killed without anger. I thought I could be angry before, I thought I would do it with great anger, but I didn't. Then I came in and I looked, she was lying there and even asked, what is it? She knew what, and she also knew that it was no use running because I would go after her. The pain of being a cuckold, a deep pain in the chest, something draining your strength from inside. I don't even know how to say it. A woman is not like a man. The man goes there and he pours himself out. The woman receives the juice of another man. And the juice stays there inside her, it mixes itself with her. Thus she is no longer the same woman. Also, she has to open herself up. And when she opens herself up like that and spreads out her limbs and shows all of herself, what secret remains? A woman who has been seen by two is different from the woman who has been seen by only one, because she has to open her legs, to show herself inside. She's not the same woman. I thought I might tell her that, I even started opening my mouth to speak. Normally I don't talk to people I shoot, it makes no sense. Who kills a hog, for instance, and keeps talking to it about how it's going to die because of this or that? It's just the knife, and nothing more. You don't talk to people you kill. But I wanted to talk to her, because when my feet first touched the floor tiles of the open room, I felt pain. As I went closer to her, the pain went away, but I couldn't speak. Those clear eyes so still and her hair pulled sideways and her head tilted, looking at me. Are you all right? She knew. When she saw I had my arm behind my back, she turned away her eyes. Again I wanted to speak. I could speak, but I was afraid to talk. If you want to do something, don't talk. If you don't, then talk. I had to do it. I didn't like to think I was going to cross the street with people looking at me: There goes the cuckold. This I could have told her. But I said nothing and when I plunged the iron, I closed my eyes. She made no sound. She fell there, with her hands on her belly. I left right away and never set foot there again. I live everywhere. Better to live walking, now. Luzinete tells me, get me with child. No woman is going to be heavy by me in this world ever again. Once that one child was killed, all the rest that might come were killed too. Enough, you sticky vine, I detest a person hanging on to me all the time, out. So I live here and there, everywhere. A man's wife is himself, not counting once in a while one thing or another, just for a discharge for relief, there being the need. I am my wife and I am my son and I am I. So it is.

And the next day they could see me dancing when they had the allegories, playing a sailor on a great ship of war, pull up the anchor, ho-ho, and set the sails. In Riachuelo. Everywhere. Tell me, isn't Sergipe the middle of everywhere? Aren't the great beauties here and the green woods, what a land. Don't we have everything here, and don't we prefer to remain here? Right? I may be the king of the Congo. Herding hogs. Doing whatever I please. Raising hell. There are times when I feel free, admiral of the moors, king of the moors, king of the moors. There I go. All the way to hell, possibly. I feel a great many things. There is a basket wobbling on the back of a mule, a basket full of clay bulls. Those grilles, I won't go back there. But a basket, panniers, a basket full of clay, a basket full of bulls, Mother, the wilted orange tree, the other trees all dead, wobbling down old Orange Tree Street among the grilled houses, a basket full of clay, a pannier full of bulls, a basket full of bulls. All is still, just that clay herd keeps going up and down with the mule's rump. Small painted eyes that don't move. Horns that don't stab. 31

Legs that don't walk. But when the sun hits the marketplace, which glitters and then wavers, the bull herd stirs. Ay, ay, ay, ay, aaaaaaaaaaay a clay bull, a clay bull, aaaaaay, ay, ay, ay, Mother, a clay bull in the mist, a clay bull in the market, on the rump of a mule. A mule with two water casks on his sides, each step a leaning to the right and a leaning to the left, two water casks for our dryness, and see how the orange tree is wilted, Mother, ay, aaaaaaay, ay a clay bull, a clay bull, a basket full of clay, full of clay bulls in the marketplace. Two cow skulls back home, many cow skulls, the white bones and our clothes full of holes and my chest gear with no frills and me sitting at the edge of nothing, my eyes glued to the eggshells they put on the tips of poles and branches. Ay a clay bull, a clay of the bull I ate, all colors. I'll die one of these days, and the wilted orange tree, ay Mother, a clay bull. I put a finger in my ear very slowly and slowly I shake it and shake it and shake it, until I let out a loud chant that flies in the air. But no one listens. There is no herd, my chant is empty. I've never been a cowhand. But even so I let out a very loud cattle chant and my finger almost pulls off my ear and I look at the ground and I am sad.

III

I thought I had a chigger in my big toe, so I tried to find it just with my eyes, but I couldn't see anything and so I spent some time thinking about the names of the worthless places in these parts, Planta de Milho, Pedra Preta, Miramar, Cocomanha, a lot of them, most of them hardly there at all, only two or three straw houses or maybe just twigs and branches, and scrawny people dragging themselves along, their faces almost touching the ground, and I ended up finding myself mindlessly staring at this big toe from up here, so I stuck my finger between the toe and the dirt and scratched softly, pinching my flesh. My foot is all flaky from wearing boots for who knows how many days, I can't even remember, and all these veins showing bluely, and when I pulled out my socks they were powdery at the tips like corn flour. Whether they think I am rude or not, I have to stretch my feet up in the direction of the roof and air everything very thoroughly, to get rid of the stench, which is most potent. But there is no place to lean your back against on this porch, so the best thing you can do is to set your feet back on the ground to look at them again, this time more closely and with great attention. And I was doing that when I felt the chigger inside my toe, a buried itch that never goes away. I pinched once again and caught the very place where it was burrowed. Not that I am in the mood to remove a chigger now, I would prefer not to do anything, maybe to roll up a cigarette in no hurry, to fix and unfix it until its shape is round in the middle and flat at the ends, and then to look at the smoke, which is very easy and good in this still air, or to stand motionless staring at that orange-colored bull that poises himself over yonder, at rest and moving his tail, he has the deportment of a fine bull. But no one can discover a chigger without feeling obliged to extract it. It stays there as though people were its pasture, it fattens on us. There is always something to compel a Christian to deviate from his law-abiding ways. And I had to take my paper of needles from under the bandolier and unfold it without letting the threads fall out and choose a needle by looking at it against the light and lick its tip again and again to draw out the infectiousness. After that, cross the legs ankle over knee for a good position and pick out the chigger with the tip of the needle. You have to break the skin but you must not break the chigger, because then a great number of them are born, like a multiplication table. This disgraceful excuse for toehide looks like the skin of a tangerine, it's falling apart. A remarkable stench, I'll have to rub lemon and ashes onto these parts, it's the only thing to do.

This devil of a pox of a girl keeps studying me from over there. Only yesterday I thought she wanted some of my tapioca pie and I gave her a pie, although there were more pies around than a man could want. I don't know why she should want mine. You want some pie? She didn't want any. I think she is too grown up to be walking around the house in her undergarments. Her body is already full. Yesterday Amaro saw it, and said, "May God bring you up, may Our Lady bless you." And he fastened his eyes on her behind, thinking mischief. I said, "Take it easy, Amaro." "Oh, nothing like that," he says. Nothing like that, nothing like that? You had better explain what nothing like that means to her father, when he notices you have intentions for his daughter. Ahn, well, that's fair warning. But he just stayed there holding a razor sedge stalk in his hand, and then cutting little pieces of it with his steel knife and then lining them up and flicking them with his finger. As if he were not even there. Well, I don't know. There are other times when she comes in her slip, one can see her breasts underneath. I don't know. This I don't like, it always turns into a disturbance. Oh well, none of my business, a motherless daughter, no brother, and the father occupied with the cows. She had a twin brother. So they say, I never saw him myself. He died of lockjaw. His navel festered, they put manure and mashed goosefoot on it, nothing worked. He became hard as wood, no man could bend him, and they buried him in a standing position. Half crouched, half standing. So they say, I never saw it myself. Who cares. What I care about is going away as soon as Elevaldo comes and says, you can go. I'll go right away. This place gives me a pain, especially with Amaro cutting razor sedge stalks, biting razor sedge stalks, cutting his finger on razor sedge stalks, a madhouse. And he doesn't take his eyes from the girl's bottom. I don't know. She is a woman already, must be about thirteen years old, maybe fourteen, her crupper is just about down to the point where she can be seen to be a woman. And there she stands, eyes screwed into me.

"You picking out a chigger, Sr. Getúlio?"

I don't like being called senhor. Why, dammit, what good are my stripes? Yes, I am picking out a chigger, what else could I be doing with a needle in my hand and my foot in the air, would I be sewing my feet? I don't like her ways, her eyes are forever moving about and her face is wily and her hands are always crumpled on her lower belly. Hell. I don't   35 like it. And the worst is that Amaro keeps watching her and grinning. The day before yesterday I caught him grinning at her and her grinning back at him. When I noticed all the shamelessness, they froze. When I arrived here, I warned everybody: Lock this character in the small room, put a pisspot in there, have Old Osonira take him food and tie him up to a beam. They did so the first day. The second day they felt sorry for him, he looks very proper with his high schooling and all. What a gentleman. And that old deaf cow, Old Osonira, keeps talking — oh the poor man with his hands cut by the rope, oh the poor man who has no strength left even to move, oh the poor man who does not even complain, oh the poor man who is so hungry. If I had my way, I would decapitate this old mare's tongue, the pox. I see no usefulness in her. She importunes people, that's what she does. And Amaro goes on talking and Nestor goes on talking. To me the older they get the more spineless they get. People say this one Nestor has a past, and events to his credit. For my part I watch him as he covers himself with leather and goes out while I remain settled here. He rounds up the cows, spends all his God-given day with the cows. He seems to have good flesh on his bones, to judge from his scorched face and his squinty eyes. When he rides back from the field, before his bath, he sits there and cleans his nails one by one with the tip of a jackknife, very, very slowly and with great deliberation. Sometimes he listens to the radio, not always. Impressive, but just the same he almost asked for the man's freedom, like Old Osonira. This I don't understand. To me this person is an animal, he is turning into a beast. And so they finally took the man out of the room, but I wouldn't let them do away with the rope. He has to be tied up like a bundle of corn, even if he has to stay in the middle of the living room, and if he wishes to walk let him walk with a rope 36   around his neck. I told Nestor, he is no good, this somebody.

I said, he is not a good thing. He is not a person. To me he is a werewolf. I said this to Nestor: This one turns into a werewolf, listen to me, this one almost turned the city of Ribeirópolis into nothing, listen to me. It didn't work. He's really a wild animal, this pox is a beast. I wish I could bleed him and finish this mission. But no, I have to take him with me, there is nothing I can do now. Now he stays in the living room, he greets everybody.

"Good afternoon to all."

What a gentleman. As though he had never given a death order, as though he had never nullified the returns of an election, as though he never felt a sin weighing on his back, how about that? That must be the reason why I seem to be the bandit here, I who never shot anybody in the back, never. And I am the bandit here. I am afraid that if this goes on much longer he will end up being let loose and I will stay here like a mad dog, with a dry corncob tied to my neck and a rope tied to my foot. Who ever heard of such a thing? There is a whip over there, a triple-belted whip, everybody knows what kind I am talking about. What am I doing, that I don't take that whip from the wall and flay him and Old Osonira and whoever comes by and whoever else comes by and resolve everything and end it? Why do I let this happen? Why don't I do anything? This is funny, to keep allowing things to happen, it's really funny. What is now building is a feeling for him and against me and even Amaro contributes his share and then goes back to his razor sedge stalks, staring at the girl's behind with the face of a dog who just broke the food pot. Oh well. So it is. I can't tolerate this, I get to be like a boiling kettle, I can't bear it.

Well, Elevaldo will come any time now, it is not possible for him not to return. He caught up with us halfway through the trip and he almost took one in his forehead, since he appeared all of a sudden and I was just burning blue to make   37 a few changes in the world, and I didn't like what he did, fumbling in the bushes without forewarning. Do you happen to know, Sr. Elevaldo, that you, senhor, were lucky that I didn't have my iron in my hand when you sprang from behind the bushes, because if I had I would not have hesitated, it would have been thunk-thunk-thunk, all in one single hole? In the middle of the forehead in a single hole and through that very same hole you would leave us. He looked at me like that. He didn't like it. Stop being funny, Getúlio. Ah-han, let him think what he likes.

"It happens that we have to keep the man on Nestor Franco's ranch for a while."

Every now and then when you are enjoying yourself the most, when you are just about ready to conclude everything, salute and turn back, something like that comes along.

"You must tell me why."

"The newspapers are making a hell of a noise, there are federal troops coming to Aracaju. The chief said on the radio that he had arrested no one."

"Actually, he didn't arrest him, it was I who arrested him."

All the while the pox is standing nearby tied up to the hog plum tree, and he guffaws. Once an aunt I used to have saw the devil standing by a jack fruit tree that she was going to chop and when she swung down the ax blade went loose and she said, this is one devil of a cheap ax, and what happens next but the very devil comes up, a filthy creature, a pitch-black creature, the worst creature ever seen, with a tail and a stench, and he said to her with the most shameless face, a face like only the devil can make:

"Did you call me?"

This he said singing in a fluty voice. It is said that the creature's breath was so bad and his gullet so ugly that it was all a complete queasiness. Pure turd. The only thing to do is to cross yourself. Think about his face, with that speech of a devil.

"Did you call me?"

Then he complained that she called that cheap ax by his name, and explained that he had nothing whatsoever to do with the loosening of the blade, and that he wasn't even doing any tempting in that place at that hour, but he was only passing by because this was the day he had to go tempting in Itaporanga, and that it wasn't a decent thing to do to call a cheap ax a devil just like that. She said she hadn't called it a devil. "I said marvel, not devil." "What do you mean you said marvel, you liar," the creature said, and then he gave her two clapping slaps to her face, I heard they were two such slaps as would make you roll on the ground, given by that pitchblack hand, a filthy hand, the kind of hand you would expect a devil to have. And he turned around pulling up her skirt and saying the worst things with a most shameless face, such as only the devil can make. She said that he said to her:

"Did you call me? My name is Erundino."

He was a different kind of devil, who was neither a Lucifer nor a Beelzebub nor a Satan nor a Belial, but was this one Erundino. And he kept doing that little dance of his: "My name is Erundino, my name is Erundino." A filthy creature, a pitchblack creature, you should see him, that particular devil. She was lucky that she remembered a prayer, my Saint Cyprian, the three crosses of David, the three signs of Solomon, the three tears of Magdalene, the three wounds of Christ, and she kept on praying, kept on praying, until she found a good position to step on the tail of the apparition, a sharp-tipped tail like an Indian arrow, and then it occurred that he detonated and vanished, nevertheless leaving a stench that stayed afloat around those wilds for over twenty years, there was no one who could pass by without reeling. 39

So when I saw the somebody let out that guffaw tied to the hog plum tree, what came to my mind was the devil my aunt had encountered. He was there grinning white-toothedly, and spoke:

"Sr. Getúlio, let's forget about all this. Look, I'll pull back to Paulo Afonso and stay in Bahia and you go wherever you wish and everything will cool down and remain in blessed peace."

Yes. To me he is an animal, I believe that. Elevaldo brought orders, there is no way to disobey. But before that I communicated with the somebody as follows:

"You, senhor, you please do not speak. As a matter of fact, I can use my rifle butt on your teeth, and I would even appreciate it if you called my mother names, so that I would have an excuse to pick up this rifle here and give you a couple of slugs in the face, what do you say?"

Perhaps Elevaldo had no say in this matter, perhaps the best thing to do is to remain here quietly, but his face gives me this desire to use violence. I don't know what it is about his face. If you had a boil in your nose, I would like to give it a swat sideways with great strength, you know, it might even do you good, a strong swat with a rifle butt is a good remedy for boils. I asked Elevaldo whether it wouldn't be better to finish the job right then and there, I even described my plans for the execution very loudly. I wanted the thing to hear everything, especially because he pretended to pay no attention to anything going on and he had a certain confidence. I said, we can hang him, this thing is worthless. Elevaldo looked at him like he was considering whether it was a good idea. That one is not a jewel either, that Elevaldo. And Amaro came out of the Hudson rubbing his face, smearing the lump he has on his forehead with spit from his empty stomach, and asked, "Isn't it true that we are about to finish this one now? Because if we are we had better hurry," Amaro said, "to put an end to all this early morning annoyance once and for all." Elevaldo said nothing, he just made a couple of throat noises. By this time, the scum stopped showing his teeth from his sitting place on the roots of the hog plum tree. Ah, so you stopped laughing, you diseased trash. You see how life is? Ahn. On second thought, hanging will mean too much work, because the rope we have in the trunk of this vehicle is too thin and is likely to cut through his neck instead of hanging him, and that would turn into a messy job. "I tell you, Sr. Elevaldo, you know about these medical things, isn't it better to give him lumpy salt until his kidneys burst? Because if you don't give the salt with a great deal of water that's what happens, although it is slow and likely to provoke whimpering. Do you think he will whimper? It is even beneficial to him, brine is good for preserving." Elevaldo just looks on, making throat noises. We'll do as follows: We'll pour honey over his parts and find a newborn calf to lick them. As the honey is licked away, we pour some more. Thus he will die prettily, laughing away. Or we'll bury him alive, head down. Or, better, both things. Salt, because it was salt that he sprinkled over the land of the Paraíbas in Ribeirópolis. A calf, because calves are what he killed, one by one. Was it so or was it not so, pox? I know it was. When you did it you were the big boss, weren't you? Now watch what I do. But it seems that Elevaldo felt sorry for him, and told us to take the man to Nestor's place and that he considered his message delivered and he would come back to tell us when to resume the trip. Maybe alongside the river, avoiding roads, it remained to be seen. We set the man on a march toward the house, and Amaro was happy, because he kept looking back from time to time and singing, march, march on, paper-headed soldier, and then he said lump-headed soldier and papaya-headed and shrimp-headed and capon-headed and jambolan-headed and so forth, until we got to the house and lodged ourselves and here I am with this girl looking at me and wishing to know about my picking out a chigger from my toe.

A dreariness here. In the beginning I used to chew on some of the fermented goat cheese they have here for lack of something to do, but now I eat only because I have to, and spend my hours lying on the porch. I don't know how many days have passed. Amaro cuts razor sedge stalks, tinkers with the motor of the Hudson and whistles the same song over and over again and sings sometimes. I don't understand the words well, because he rolls his tongue and nothing of meaning comes across. Even the sun, he says. I understand that: Even the sun. Even the sun isptease her invaded the window-pane and inspurled-ah her picture. Let me examine this. Even the sun isptease her invaded the windowpane and inspurled-ah her picture. I wonder what the shit that is. I asked him. Even the sun isptease her, what does that mean? I don't know, he said, that's the way I learned it. And inspurled-ah her picture. I think songs should be made to be understood, not like this. Amaro knows several of them, but he has the custom of picking one and never letting it get away from his mouth, and he goes on and on all day.

> Lovely doll
> With blond hair
> And temptatrix eyes
> And lipsions a lubil.

I asked him what in the world were lipsions a lubil, and he didn't know either. It appears that he doesn't like me to ask. I think it makes no sense to sing something you don't understand, and I told him so, but he wouldn't hear of it. Lipsions a lubil, lipsions a lubil, I never heard that before. He's the only one who says that. Normally I wouldn't care, but when all you have to listen to is the mooing of cows and all you have to smell is the smell of bullpens and you don't know when this stupefaction is going to end, it's really hard to put up with something like that. Amaro likes words. He keeps repeating a number of them to himself like a madman, I think he just enjoys their taste. Before I started picking out the chigger, before I even started to untie my boots, he came around and said, with a piece of razor sedge stalk between his teeth:

"If we take the man to Aracaju now, there will be a potheosis of gunfire."

Now, now just listen to that. Is that so. When he spoke I almost felt like laughing, especially because Amaro has one tooth here and one tooth there, he'll end up losing them all. His mouth is funny, like the jagged teeth you can carve out of a watermelon rind. Nothing to do. There is nothing else to do, except perhaps whittle away a watermelon rind, and when time is as large as here and stretches itself through the afternoon as though it would never come to an end, even conversation sounds like a thing from hell, it brings on impatience. Amaro either talks about women or he talks about Charuto, the Cotinguiba soccer forward. He talks about Charuto's kick. What a kick, he says. What kicks. The ball ripped through the net against the Passagem team, it left its mark there. He ripped many nets, he did this and that. All right, Amaro, ahn-well, I don't like the Cotinguiba team. In the first place I don't like their town, which is a shriveled-up little place, full of juveniles escaped from the reformatory, in the second place I don't like blue-shirted teams, in the third place I don't think that Charuto, with his stork legs and his pointed nose, can be a good kicker, in the fourth place shut that goddamned, babbling mouth of yours, you hear, the only real team is Olímpico, you hear? Good. I never even paid any attention to the Olímpico uniform, I can only re-   43 member those wheels intertwined inside each other on the chests of the players, but I have to say something, what else is there to do? At first comes a little annoyance at Amaro, the holes in his teeth and his drawling Muribecan speech, but then time is so large and nothing can be heard but the cows and the heat is so smothering and nothing else can be heard that we stay there, talking just for talking, among great standstills in the conversation, while we look at the air. Lying on an old cot at night, sleepless, we have an aimless talk. What else? And Amaro says only Charuto this and Charuto that, because Charuto, because of more of this and more of that. All right, all right. At times some white frogs appear on the floor and we watch the frogs as though we had never seen a frog in all our lives and we use the opportunity to discuss frogs without much direction. Like this: Amaro says, "Have you noticed how white these frogs are, see how white these creatures are." At that I raise my head from the cot, close one eye because of the glare of the lamp, and watch the frog. I spend some time considering the frog, which sits there without cares, no doubt waiting for some firefly. Then I say to Amaro: "You are right, it is one hell of a white creature, just thinking about it you couldn't imagine a creature so white." Then he nods and says: "It is such a white little creature that it looks as though someone painted it, huh?" Then I raise my head once again, look at the frog and say: "It almost does seem someone painted it, such is the whiteness of this frog, huh Amaro?" "How true," Amaro says. "A whiteness such as this can only come from painting." Then he watches the frog some more and I watch too, and every time each one of us says something just slightly different. It is white. Under the light, you can see its bowels. The firefly lights up inside its belly when it swallows one. After that the firefly starts losing its illumination and gets dimmer and dimmer until it goes out. Amaro says that the frog is a relative of the toad.

44

"Everybody knows that, Amaro. Tell me, isn't this Hudson going to stall in the middle of the road?" "What do you mean, stall, what do you mean, holy saints?" "This Hudson is American, isn't it, Amaro?" "I saw two Americans once, they were red. Are there any blacks over there?" "There are not. Bahia is not in America." "America is beyond Africa, it is very far." And we go on like that for a long time, until I feel like practicing some shooting on the frog, and Amaro says it is going to cause an excessive number of holes in the floor and will provoke an unacceptable noise. For that reason we fastened our eyes on the frog and it remained frogging motionlessly and quietly and we didn't shoot it and ended up having to go to sleep in that sweltering quietness. Amaro found a brown book and applied himself to read it. It had a sentence: The verbless speech. But he didn't like the speech and pretty soon he rolled down the lamp wick with his big toe and went to sleep. I figure he is dreaming of a frog inside the Hudson.

Now that I have this chigger at the tip of the needle, I can burn it with a match. It doesn't even flinch, there is no time for that. What does happen to it is a twisting curling sideways, zh-zh, a little outstretching and it gets all charred. It leaves a good-sized hole, I can assure you, and it is necessary to stuff earth into it so as to make it disinfect. Sometimes I get very angry when I see myself doing certain things, a man like me sitting here and rubbing dirt into a hole in his big toe, knowing he will have nothing to do afterward. I could go out with Sr. Nestor, but I don't get along well with cows. I don't like the company of cattle, they are stupid animals and carry their heads low. Besides, I can't leave him alone here with this girl strutting around him, because she might set him free, I am sure of this. But one thing is certain, if she sets him free I'll shoot her.

I noticed nothing until the bedlam broke out. I am sitting   45 here minding my own business, scratching my punctured toe, when I hear screams in the living room and the screams come from Old Osonira, help me Our Lady of Perpetual Help, help me Good Jesus of Pirapora, and tattle-tattle, tattle-tattle, and there she is all ruffled up, so when I see so much craziness on the part of Osonira I burst through the door already holding my barrel in the direction of where he could run to, I enter with my steel pointing out ahead, and what I see is the girl holding her parts with her hand and cowering as though someone were trying to catch her, and the somebody all messed up and exposed in front. As soon as I saw it, I stopped.

"I am telling you, Sr. Nestor, if I had a knife in my hand I would have cut it right off. It was a scandal."

Well, actually it wasn't quite like that because I did have my boot knife and it was a good knife, too. But I saw no sense in doing that. The man was still tied up but he had found a way to open himself in front and now what he was about to do was to relieve himself with the girl. And the only reason he did not get what he intended and had to remain with his hammer swaying in the wind was that the sheath slipped away when Old Osonira showed up. Nobody could have predicted that, because the poxy old woman should have already trudged her league and a half back to her house, but on that day she took it into her mind to stay and so she caught the shamelessness.

"Look, Sr. Nestor, the fact is that the girl did not want to do it, and he was going to do it by force."

The fact is that she was all for it, she must have been the one who opened him up, because his hands couldn't move well in that state of tiedness. But she drew back and started crying and sobbing: She didn't want it, she told her father, she went to give him water and he grabbed her, she is a maiden and stays quietly in her place without bothering anyone.

"It's a fact, Senhor Nestor. The girl was sitting quietly in her place. The bastard is bad, to me he is an animal."

Yes. I'll bet good money that she was the one who started it. Ahn-well, shoo. No one wants someone and gives him up for no reason. I am here and I am watching and I can't promise I didn't enjoy seeing Sr. Nestor shake his head from one side to the other studying the man's lack of composure. And the man not knowing what face to make nor whether to look up or look down, whether to bite his lip or not, whether to speak or not, whether anything.

"Take your hands away from your front there, pestilent thing. Didn't you want to show it? Well, go ahead and show it."

It was all shrunk up, as you would guess. I wouldn't want to be in his place. But Sr. Nestor just said a couple of things aloud and struck the girl with his hand and Amaro and I went over to help hold the girl, so that he could hit her once or twice. She deserved it. A woman who has seen a man in such a state is a whore. Or will be. Punishment does good. That is the reason why we held her a little, as her father punished her thoroughly with the same whip I was looking at before, and caught the leather with his left hand. That is to say, she would get it on the way down and on the way up. But there was no need to hold her any longer, because that whip was of the kind used to tame mules, so that she cringed and stood still. He handled the whip well, barely moving his arm and just using his wrist, almost. He hit well. Old Osonira went out and came back with vinegar and salt for the welts. It was necessary. No man can be fond of a daughter like that, even if he figures it is not her fault. Damn women, they should have no say about anything, period. 47

Besides, vinegar and salt are fast healers, only a few red spots are left, all will be forgotten tomorrow, believe me. Now the thing to do is not to say a word and thank heaven for having a good father, who decided not to throw her out to follow the career of a whore. I knew all the time that this was bound to come out of it, all that flirting. That slip with nothing underneath. After all, get a naked woman and a naked man together and one of them will end up on top of the other, that's a known fact.

As soon as things calmed down, Sr. Nestor called both of us for a talk on the porch, I rolling up a cigarette and Amaro digging the ground with the tip of his boot and making a long line, and Sr. Nestor holding a knife. I said, as far as I am concerned you could bleed him right away, but the bleeding will have to be done in Aracaju. This is a fancy kind of animal, full of ideas. He can't die out in the wilds. Come to think of it, I'm not sure even about Aracaju, he is resourceful. He is very important, there's a whole system, the newspapers, everything. Politics is changing, I said, it is turning into a prissy politics. But Sr. Nestor wasn't listening, because he answered nothing at all, so I shut my mouth and remained waiting, right there. Also, there was little else to do, one had to wait. And wait we did, because he was not in a hurry, he had to do much thinking about what he should do. If someone was nervous, it wasn't me or anybody else, it was the one in the living room who instead of sitting down kept walking as far as the rope would let him. In the beginning he wanted to speak, he set up an argument.

"You must listen to me, my very dear sir. This is a problem that can be explained."

"Go explain in your slutmother's house," Sr. Nestor said, and he got up, went over there to the man and pumped his knee twice on the man's balls. "This way you will quiet down, I am not about to argue with a cheap bastard such as you, you hear." He came back and sat in the wicker chair and started rocking rhythmically, staring hard straight ahead. "You can send the girl to Saint Joseph's Convent," Amaro said. "It is purifying. She comes out old and weak-memoried. Or else send her to one of those that have bars and she can only talk through the bars and also cannot see anybody, I think."

"If I had it my way she would die, Sr. Amaro. To me she does not exist."

Ahn-well, everybody silent then, whose daughter was she after all? He took some more time and only then demonstrated his thinking.

"It is impossible to kill the man, somebody might come here. And that would start people into backbiting me, and I can't stand that."

Right, right. We can beat him up.

"On second thought, I'll leave him one-balled. Will you do the burning?"

"I never burned even a goat's balls, let alone that."

"There is no difficulty. You just put the hot iron against it. There is a certain smell of charred beef, but it is necessary, because if you don't burn there may be too much bleeding and the creature dies of drainage. Thus you burn it right off and it heals in a fine way."

Amaro said you could tie a hair from a horse's tail to the balls' roots, because then it goes on strangling and strangling, until the balls get to be like fluffy dough. "Exactly," Sr. Nestor said, "but he can pull the hair out at a time of carelessness when no one is looking." "But it is better," Amaro said, "it is the best way to cut out warts, it doesn't even hurt, it only discomforts you a little. When you cut your hand may slip, and if you slice right through you may do too much damage. No man will sit still at a time like that." 49

"We'll warn him: Look, if you make any noise I'll stuff a piece of cloth into your mouth and you might suffocate right there. Better be resigned to it, because fate makes no mistakes. Also cease twitching, because it makes it difficult. Leave it to me, I'll do the job with just one cut at the root, in just one little moment."

"You can also pound it with a heavy mortar's pestle, and you don't even have to wrap it, as it possesses a natural wrapping. One can go on pounding and pounding until it gets powdery inside and then you leave it alone, as it swells and gets puffed up. It becomes a most impressive pouch, it may come down to one's knees. I know of an old man in Aquidabã by the name of Manoel Joaquim who has one like that, the right one, which is the exact image of a squash of the long kind, and he can do his chores mindless of it, only his pant legs have to be a bit wider to hold it. I have seen it several times, it's very interesting. There is nothing to do in Aquidabã, and Sr. Manoel Joaquim enjoys long conversations and he sits there with that bloated ball inside his pants like a sandbag. But that came from a disease, not from blows. It's a disease there is, that swells your balls and then there's nothing you can do about it."

"No, because he may pass out and not recover. Or he may become feeble-minded for the rest of his life."

Now, for somebody who just a little while ago flushed all over, really in heat, to see the old man's blade so well honed it would sing while flashing in his hand and ready to separate a nut from the creature, for this somebody not to kneel down he must be very much a man. But not him. I observed that he was pretending to be very tired, as if nothing had anything to do with him. He was just there, I think if someone told him to kneel down he would have, and if someone told him to spread apart his behind he would have. He is an animal, believe me. Would you say National Democrats are people?

And we went on considering the ways to deball the man, one ball coming out so he would learn, and one ball staying so he would remember, but we found some defect with every method, either because of the bleeding or because of the consequences or because of the questions they were going to ask when he got to Aracaju. I myself see nothing wrong with a National Democrat arriving one-balled in Aracaju. I speak for myself, but there are those who would not think well of it. To me he is an animal, it makes no difference. He is over there, sometimes stopping and standing still, his head up like a horse's. There were times it seemed the conversation had nothing to do with him, and there were times he rubbed his hands together but said nothing, indicating that he must have concluded it would be best to turn mute.

"If you go on like that you will castrate the man before it's time to."

"This will warm him up," Sr. Nestor said. "It is a preparation. It is a good thing to have him feel it beforehand, because in this house the only man who draws out his rod to do something other than pissing is I. I don't like this whole business, I can't tolerate this lack of respect."

"Rightly so."

But it was already the middle of the night and the crickets and frogs were everywhere and no one had made up his mind about anything. My obligation is to deliver the prisoner whole.

"You, senhor, you forgive me, but he can't go out of here whole. Ask him if he ever thought of leaving the girl whole. If it hadn't been for Old Osonira he'd have gone deep into it, he'd have made a carnival out of it."

Well, the thing to do is to find another way. "Hey Amaro, 51 if you hit somebody's head against the glass windows of the car, does the glass shatter?" Amaro said, "Ho-hum, it doesn't shatter, it yields like taffy, it can even crack a little but it won't shatter very easily, that's American glass." Then I know what to do. We say that the man hit his head against the glass when we ran over a couple of bumps on the road. So any damage to his face will be explained. Let him tell them it wasn't the bumps, because that will be the last thing he'll ever say. "Do you have pliers in the house? If so I'll pull two front teeth off him. I'll pull out two lower teeth and two upper teeth to make things even. This way he'll be able to spit and whistle well, huh? First I'll hit him with the rifle butt on the lips to deaden the pain and to soften things up and to make him open his mouth more easily. Then I pull once, I pull twice, I pull thrice and I pull out. There is no difficulty in it. The lower ones you pull straight up, and the upper ones you pull straight down. If it resists, you swing from one side to the other until it gives up." Sr. Nestor brought in a tin trunk covered with rust, so much that it groaned when opened, and gave me the pliers. They weren't much better than the trunk, black with rust. I thought they would be likely to wreck his gums. "I think they are going to wreck your gums, thing. You forgive me, senhor, but there is no other way, it is either this or caponification. Be understanding about this, all right, friend?

"Do you happen to know a fancy word for pulling out teeth? Would you be so kind as to open your little daisy of a mouth quick? Dammit, damn you!"

Then I turned my weapon around, pounded twice on the creature's lips and pulled out four teeth with the pliers, and stopped.

IV ♘

I never could have imagined that Amaro knew these prayers
or that this Japoatã priest was going to make the three of us
kneel down to pray. I did not know the priest. I used to know
him only by name, and when I saw him I thought he was not
a priest, I thought he was some deranged man playing priest.
Or he could also be possessed. He speaks fast and deep, so
you almost don't understand what he says. But one can see
why he is known as the Priest of Steel with the Red Face,
because he lets his toughness show and because he has a red
spot across his face, which gets now redder and then less red
and so it goes, accordingly. He knew we were arriving and
he had to give us shelter, but he stood all kinglike at the door
with his arms crossed, and it was eleven in the evening and
we had been out in the world for who knows how many
hours. He peeked from behind some wooden bars in the
middle of the church's side door. And he kept on peeking
and making no sign, with Amaro and me all worn out and
having to drag that piece of junk along and showing our
gaping mouths by the door. Besides we were disguised in
hooded overcoats and the creature was gagged behind us

groaning because of the pain of the gag on his gums, since the pliers were not the kind specifically for pulling out teeth and they were rusty and slippery, so that the extraction was delayed and the gums almost came out with the teeth and we spent a great deal of time fearing he would die without the expected punishment, and there was some nervousness because it was not the time for jokes, what with a dead and beheaded lieutenant and a lot of men in the shootout and a complete mess back at Sr. Nestor's farm, and all this the priest knows and just stands there with his arms crossed. Why, no matter whether he is a priest or a friar, a nun or a bishop, a saint or an angel, an image or a prophet, he has no right to stand there just watching at a time like this for such a long time it seems like a year. It doesn't seem like a year. Rather, it seems like a day, for a year goes by quickly, but a day goes by slowly. I decided to watch too, holding my gun handle in my hand and leaning my head against his bars, but he didn't back away from them, he just lifted a votive candle to light his face, which was not a good face, but a face all red, a red and lumpy face, full of pockmarks. He looked like a devil, glaring at us like that. But we stood eye to eye, without moving. And I popped my eye as open as I could, so I could face him well. I threw back the hood and put my face to the light and gave the creature a pull, come here junk, all you know how to do is to groan under that gag, learn the manner of a man, look at the priest, ask for the priest's blessing. The creature was a little stupefied with what was going on, it all seemed to have taken hours. The priest ended up by saying, "Anybody out there, anybody out there," with a voice like a cave. He had something like a nightcap on his head, I don't know what the devil it was, an appurtenance of a priest. "Anybody in there," I said, "anybody in there, anybody in there?" Getúlio, of course. Getúlio of Acrísio Antunes, Antunes of the Social Democrats, Social Democrats of this Sergipe, Sergipe of this mighty world, mighty world that is getting hot, getting hot and it's going to melt, oh shit, senhor priest, hey you priest, why don't you open this shit of a door, are you going to open it or do we have to take off for Pacatuba or Pirambu, but if the mission is a failure you will be the failure. The priest is crackbrained, believe me. Anybody out there, anybody out there? Anybody in there, anybody in there! Do you want me to ring the bell? Anybody at home, anybody in church? "Is Nestor dead," the priest asked, without opening the door. "He won't die easily," I said, "but I think he is bringing an end to a heap of people over there, I think there is high mortality in the Ranch of Good Hope, because they tried to go in by force. But I'll tell you all about it, why don't you open the door?"

"In the name of God," said the priest, opening the door.

We went in and there was a black dog and the nightcapped priest in a flowing nightshirt, carrying a two-barreled, sawed-off instrument hanging from a strap over his shoulder, with the two hammers pulled back. He supported it between his armpit and his elbow, aiming straight ahead. I never saw one just like it, "Sr. Priest, tell me, aren't these two hammers pulled back?" "They are," said the priest, "and if you bump against it they come down and we are going to have a couple of loud bangs. There is a good load in there; I think if you hit them both at once it will throw a good-sized male back maybe four armlengths." "And wouldn't you say, senhor, you should push back those hammers very gently onto the caps? I tell you, it must deliver a punch of some two hundred kilos or more." The priest stroked the side of the machine slowly, placed his thumb on both hammers and pushed them forward carefully, making a little grimace, and relaxed his aim. "Even so," he said pointing the barrels to the floor, "it can still shoot if you press the triggers with a little force. The hammers go up and down like that of a revolver. 55

But I cannot do any shooting inside a church, because then it would cease to be a church. You don't kill inside a church, you do your killing outside. There are however many people still around who are fond of surrounding churches, so that you can't take chances, one thing I can't stand is people who surround churches. There was a time when they had elections in churches," the priest said, "and then, then you needed a lot of preparation," the priest said, sticking the two barrels of the shotgun into the hole in the back of a pew and leaving it there. He looked as though he was talking to himself, looking up and down, more up than down.

"A shot from this thing in here will bring everything falling down. There will be nothing left. I have no money to fortify it."

He spent some time that way, his hand on the dog's head and talking to himself, there is no money for this and no money for that.

"Screw it," the priest said, raising his straightened arms sideways and clapping them back down against his loins. "Everybody down to pray."

Everybody came down on their knees, I really never thought Amaro knew all these prayers, I myself don't know any. Amaro starts a loud prayer. "Shut up," said the priest, "I am the only one who can say them aloud." First we had to ungag the creature. Amaro wanted to do it slowly, as the gag seemed to be glued to the gums, but there would be no end to that if he kept it up. If I had my way I wouldn't take it off, I don't think he'll be able to talk anyway, not even to pray, his snout is all swollen from the operation, and why should he pray anyhow, since God is against National Democrats, I always say, the Communists have no God. But Amaro went on taking it off, and the creature just whining and whining. Furthermore the thing didn't smell good, it was a really disgraceful stench, and the priest held up the candle in order to take a better look at the face of the creature. "I'd better pull it out all at once," Amaro said, "because that way it's a faster pain." The priest thought we would draw blood that way, and pressed the creature's cheeks to peek inside. "What happened to this poor wretch here, Sergeant?" "Hum. Something from outside, senhor. Yes, yes. That's right." "What did you do there, Sergeant?" Holy Virgin. "Well, firstly I hit him with the rifle butt so he would open his mouth. Then I pulled out two upper teeth and two lower teeth. It was a fast job." "Hum-hum," said the priest, "you will tell me about it later. *Oremus confiteoday omnipotente beateh Marieh sempervirgi beatomicaeli arcanjo beato Jones Batista sanctis apostis Pedro et Paulo omnibussantis etibipatte cuia pecaviminis cogitatione verbetopere mea culpa mea culpa orare promeh adidomino deunostri amain.*" The creature crossed himself with both hands, since they were tied up together, which means that one of the crosses came out backward, and it's none of my affair, let him go into damnation by himself. *"Indugentum absolutonein et remissione pacatorum nostroro tributinobis omnipotes et misericordia dominus."* Many prayers. I prayed two Lord's Prayers and two Hail Marys and then I didn't feel like praying anymore, so I went on listening to the priest talking priest language. I only hope he won't make the animal well again, but I don't think this priest is the sort who makes miracles, all he can do is pray, so I sat on the pew and waited for the end of the praying and also felt like going to sleep, but I didn't know if the church would cease to be a church if I slept in it, so I managed to keep my eyes open. Amaro is a wonder, engrossed in the prayers. That must be the reason he has never had a collision in a car, he surrounds himself with prayers. I wish I knew how to pray like that. I remember the chief's son whom I took to have his first communion picture taken, he was holding up a candle with a ribbon around his arm, and the picture was taken with angels behind, but his mother didn't like it, 57 because he came out standing at attention. Who cares. He stood at attention because he felt like it, he was the one who wanted it.

The priest said, smoothing his nightshirt, the red-faced priest walking among the pews, a swimminglike gait like a cowherder's, and meanwhile the pox is all unkempt and bedraggled and his wrists are scuffed from the vine I used to tie him, and I am tired as hell. "Well," the priest said after praying for the forgiveness of our sins, "we are going to put water and salt in the poor wretch's mouth and set him up together with yourselves in the little room in the upper floor." As for myself I might as well fall down on one of these pews, but the sexton most likely comes in in the early morning to start tidying up for the first mass and I would not want to tie up a sexton too for it might bring on disgrace. "Well," the priest said, "I will show you the room; there are two leather beds and a red cement floor on which you can lay a mat, there is always a way." I would topple over right there if I could, and I keep looking at this priest, I don't know how old he might be, he may be fifty, he may be one thousand, walking like a cowherder, he must have been the son of a cowherder before being a priest, a tree of a man with no more room to grow, he even stoops a little, and I also glanced at the creature and his swollen snout. Now he was showing his back, a perfect position for a few clubbings, well, ahn-well, why shit, I don't understand it well, sometimes this priest acts like a priest, sometimes he acts like a sugar mill owner, I can't tell, and he's likely to keep conversing all night and the worst thing is that he's a high-class political person. I don't know, such tiredness. "We'll think about it tomorrow, Sergeant. Help the patient up." "How's that again, Sr. Priest?" "Help the patient up." And that was when I laughed because I really found the creature to have the face of a patient and I kept on laughing with a tickle in my belly that almost brought pain, I kept finding everything very funny and I even stroked the junk's skull and gave him a little shove. Come on, you patient, doctor patient, hey. Doesn't he really look like a patient? I feel like treating him as if he were an animal, oah patient, what a laugh, brother, ho-ah, what a laugh, ouch. The patient, can you imagine, he is a perfect patient. By this time if he could have killed me he would have. Which means therefore that he cannot live any longer, because I cannot exist with a man thirsty for my blood, it's self-evident. Now, if I could have avoided applying salt and water to the creature I would have, but we stopped in front of the water pot and then the priest decided that holy water would be better. Amaro went for it taking with him a white metal pot, the same kind of metal used in pisspots, only this pot was taller, and the priest mixed the water with salt slowly and we put water and salt on him and put it on and put it on and later on we also took him to piss, which he asked for, and then we sat him down on the mat with more vine tied around his feet. And there he remained, very well installed. Huh Amaro, you saw how this priest walks swimming downward like a cowherder? Hum-hum. Do you get along well with leather beds? We have no frogs here. Tell me, didn't your asshole tighten up when you saw the government's weaknesses arriving back there on Nestor's farm, armed like a complete expedition, did you see that, it was a crowd of real men, huh Amaro? One day you will find out, Amaro, you pox, that if you keep sleeping this soundly someone will come and do the same thing to you that that woman from Campo do Brito did to her husband, that is to say, bleed you as you snore in your hammock. After she did it, she called the foreman, whom she had been going to bed with for some time, and together they arranged the man's body in the hammock, put a washbasin underneath him and bled him like a chicken, and he became so white you had to

59

see it to believe it. I didn't see it, of course, but the chief told me about it, everybody knows about it. Now, one of these days, you being so absent-minded, someone will come and take care of you, and don't think there is no one wishing to bring you to an end, because there is, just because you drive that Hudson with me inside. Hey Amaro, that Hudson is at the church door, and what if the force shows up here? I was tired but I no longer am. I think I will load the priest's two-barreled machine and set it up at the window. One of us should remain awake, that's what we should do. Oh son of a mare, oh son of one mother and twenty fathers, oh condemned one, do you not think that by this time a band of bastards is coming over to get us? I don't know what's happening in Aracaju, Elevaldo didn't tell us clearly, but something is going on, so that for me this trip is already too long, as far as I am concerned we should get away from here, ask for the priest's blessing, wrap up the patient — hey Amaro, doesn't he look like a patient? Patient, patient, Sr. Patient, this priest is an odd one, did you see how he said screw it? You think screw means something in priest language? We wrap up this patient, stuff him in the back of the car all vined up and get out. If you asked me, I would tell you we should wait for a word in Barra dos Coqueiros and should not talk about this any longer. Over there no one will look for us, I think, because no one will think we will be right across the river from Aracaju, carrying this junk right in front of the city right by the Emperor's Bridge, looking at the crabs by the brink of the water. Maybe tomorrow, I don't know. All right, this priest knows his arts, you never know. He may use a pair of prayers, he may use that two-barreled one. I like that one, he sawed it himself and it's very well sawed, it packs over two hundred kilos, it can kill an ox, believe me. Well, if anybody arrives I insist on waiting behind the door
of the house, which is next to the church but is not the

church. I will wait right behind the door and let the first living thing that comes through have it, and it is going to be a first-class perforation, hey prickhole, ta-ta-boom, two hammers, click-click, just hit them. Did you see what huge hammers? That's an old piece, that doesn't fail, doesn't choke, looks like it has pounds and pounds of lead inside, or then it's not lead, it's a special cartridge which is even worse, I never fired an instrument such as that. Oh life, oh life, isn't this one devil of a life, Amaro? Never a quiet moment. I don't know how to do anything else either, what the hell can I do? Whoreshit, Amaro, you go to sleep so easily I can't stand it. I think this priest knows how to say a few prayers, but probably he knows only prayers against cattle sores. Of course I have never seen a priest saying cattle sore prayers, I hear it does no good. It does no good because a priest, being no cowhand, does not need it, but a cowhand needs it, so he prays and the maggots fall off one by one, thunk-thunk-thunk. Tell me, isn't Sergipe one big backland? Isn't it? The land, the life, senhor. I don't know, this leather bed hurts my backbone, doesn't it hurt yours? Nobody does any talking, I think I'm the one who does the most talking, but you can believe me when I tell you that if you go on this way you'll kick the bucket the first day God allows. Did you see the priest's dog? I used to have a dog like that, I mean, a dog more or less of the same make only thicker, whose name was Tell-You-Later, because when people asked me his name I'd say Tell-You-Later and shut up. Then a little time went by and the person would return asking the dog's name. And I would say, Tell-You-Later. Some more time, and the person would say, didn't you say you were going to tell me the dog's name, what is the dog's name, and I would say Tell-You-Later. Man, you don't even laugh, not even a laugh, who ever heard a thing like that, the moment you lie down you're fast asleep. I think you would sleep even in a trap if there were 61 one big enough, I think anybody who cares to can catch you in a trap. Amaro, you're a fool, well tonight I won't sleep well. Amaro, you stupid bird.

I don't even know how we were able to leave Good Hope in the middle of all that crossfire, it looked like Saint John's Day. Although it was all calm before, and no one could tell by Nestor's face that there was an emergency at that hour, because he arrived and dismounted and went in the house and took off all his leathers and hung them slowly and when he came out on the porch he looked at his feet and saw that he still had his spurs on, so he went back in, took off his spurs, came back out, crouched down, got up, picked some tobacco from the straw pouch, shredded it and said, "You know?" I who had nothing on my mind, and Amaro who was lying under the Hudson and I can be sure he was asleep since he had nothing to do on the car, and the prisoner was locked again in the room, what could I possibly know? Nothing. Nestor only said, "You know?" And he changed his face and stayed there. I didn't say anything and remained looking at his countenance, until he finally finished chopping his tobacco and informed me that he had some twenty men out there and that he had sent Carmolino out to the fields to gather them together and there were machetes and shotguns and a couple of short weapons, something like that, and could I wait and go out the back way after the force came? "There is a force on the way, what the hell do you mean?" "Elevaldo didn't say," Nestor said, "but I think politics are taking a contrary turn, and they sent for the man." "This one?" "The very same." "Well, we kill the man, period, they take him back stiff and unfolded, and that will be the end of that." But Nestor, who thought it was very inconsiderate of those people to barge onto his land just like that, decided that everyone should wait until the force came up to the
62   crossroads. Then we would put up a resistance, until there

was time for us to slip out to seek shelter with the Priest of Steel. "Ahn-well," Nestor said, rising with a burning cigarette in his mouth and a cloudy face, "let us welcome the government's pigs." I can't remember how long we stared down the road, and while Nestor chopped some more tobacco he started farting all over, loud farts. "I shit in my pants every time I face a showdown," Nestor said. "I am like that, I get a tremendous flux. Last time I had to defend these lands I shitted all over myself, it even seeped through my pants." Why, shoo, one shot, one fart, the more you live, isn't it? A valiant man like that jumped in front of the bullets, and shot and farted, shot and farted, wet-farted until you could see through his pants. That's odd, because the most I feel is a tightening of the chest, and even that just the moment before. In the heat I can't even see.

I never thought I was going to behead the lieutenant, at least I never thought about it clearly, I mean, I never said: "Getúlio, let's cut off this nuisance of a lieutenant's head." I hadn't even noticed he was a lieutenant until he came near, but I also saw that he was more of a bastard than anything else. We were just hanging around the place, everybody thinking something a little bit different and with an eye on the road. At times like that there is a silence; the air becomes hard, more or less. Far away a few spiked bushes, everything very quiet, only motuca flies now and then, bugs of that sort, little things like that. At that point I had never thought of beheading the lieutenant, I had never even practiced a beheading before, only he came with a white handkerchief and spoke to Nestor as if he were giving orders to one of those monkeys of his. He looked at me: You are out of uniform, Sergeant. Meanwhile I am recognizing him, and his name is Amâncio and he is exceedingly vicious and a National Democrat, everybody knows that. The sun was striking very hard and he rubbed the handkerchief around inside his cap and 63 took to squinting at us with his small eyes of a pig. He speaks with a sharp voice. I could never tolerate that type of voice in a man, although he is a very malignant sort, maybe on account of his voice. He looked at me and said, "This undisciplined sergeant took a man out of Paulo Afonso and took refuge on your land and I came to get the man, the sergeant and the driver, the government does not put up with these irregularities. The man comes along." Nestor wrinkled up his whole face. I think he was already trying to hold his urge to fart again, but he didn't say anything for a long time, although the lieutenant kept speaking and taking out a stemwinder from his pocket and striking important-looking poses and saying he had no time to waste, when Nestor suddenly spat out some pieces of chewed tobacco and started going poit-poit with his mouth until he picked out every little piece of tobacco. Then he asked the lieutenant, "Are you from the government of Bahia, senhor? For if you are thus disturbed because they took a man out of Paulo Afonso it is because you are from the government of Bahia, isn't that a fact?" "No," the lieutenant said, "I am from this government right here, your government and this sergeant's government." "Not mine," Nestor said. "Only at times. At times it is not." "Well, I am from the government that matters," the lieutenant said. "Oh," Nestor said, and let out a fart. All the while he is looking at the ground, and it is known that when a man like Nestor talks to a fellow looking at the ground it is only with the intention of not letting the other man see in his eyes what he is going to do next. I was standing by. I was silent. The land was not mine, only the hide was, and that pox was no sweet-smelling flower; there must be a lot of people spread out along the sides of the road. Nestor leaned against the wooden gate and said, "You do see this gate, don't you? Well this gate is the gate of my private road, which leads to my house, and the only people who can go

64

inside my house are the people I invite, and no one invited you." One could almost smell the smell of corpses, there were more bad men scattered around than I don't know what. "I have nothing to do with that," the lieutenant said. "I came here to pick up three men and I will not leave without them." "What men, my dear friend?" "I already told you, I explained it, rendering it very well explained, they are the sergeant, the driver and the prisoner." "Well," I said, "I don't think I'll go, do you think you will, Amaro?" "Not me," Amaro said, "I don't feel like traveling." "So there," Nestor said. "So there you are. You heard them say clearly that they do not wish to leave and I am not about to tell my guests to leave, my father gave me a good upbringing. Now, there is one thing I would like to ask of you, and this thing is, please do not go in, because if you go in you become a guest and I never shot a guest, you know how it is," Nestor said, and farted some more. Up and around you could almost hear the men taking guesses on who would get it first. God. "I know you came with a fully armed government weakness, but I hold it to be true that not even that bastard of a boss you have will give his approval to your entering the home of a decent person in this fashion and purporting to remove this person's guests from his home, to say rude things and to make trouble." "Look, Sr. Nestor, we do not want any mortality. You turn in the men and I go away and everything is in holy peace and everyone forgets the whole thing."

"In my opinion this is going to be a festival for the buzzards," Nestor said.

"That may be," the lieutenant said. "But you must remember that this khaki uniform is very hard on the buzzard's beak."

"As far as clothes go, maybe," Nestor said. "But leather is harder."

"Maybe," the lieutenant said. "But when you are in the

company of a sergeant who is a cuckold and a deserter with a queer for a driver, I cannot very well believe that."

I don't know who fired first, whether it was I or Nestor or one of the men who were lying around, but the situation couldn't possibly go on, with the lieutenant starting to whistle and those whistles seeming to be signals to the force and nobody knowing how many he had brought along with him and him calling me names I don't like, so that everything became dusty all of a sudden and we dropped behind the other side of the ditch in the middle of all the thunderclaps, and all the time Nestor kept getting up, firing his gun standing, yelling and messing up his pants more and more, he looked like a hopping monkey. Everything was blue, a big smoke, but the son of a bitch at first escaped the six shots in a row I directed at him with my left hand on the ground, and he got pinned between two trees, surrounded on all sides, although the force was behind him and sustained a great deal of fire. But I had decided I would go out there, what else could I do. In the beginning it is so: A coldness in the belly, a tightening. Then a wish not to do anything, memories. Until anger comes up to your head or some such thing, until something cracks and you let go. You really let go. So I looked for a way to close in on him, and Nestor ordered a few men to go up and around, crossing over behind our heads, to surround us and stay between us and the force, coming up from behind some bushes where no one expected. I don't know very well, but it was a brutal fire, almost one single roar, in one piece, a noise thick as stone, an undivided noise. There were plenty of leaves flying. That curtain of leaves flew in the middle of all the shooting, and I keep getting closer to the lieutenant, dragging myself alongside him, and he almost gets me, but Nestor lifts his hand and pours a rain of lead on him that made dirt go up and down on all sides and I proceed a little farther and roll over and then I watch his face, which is very close to my own with a handkerchief around the nose no doubt because of all the dust that's flying about and then I pick up a handful of dirt and throw it in his eyes and throw more and more and keep piling on dirt, when he draws a dagger that he had on his hip, he draws this jackass-sized dagger and slices the air out in front of him with his eyes closed, but in an arch that goes not only up and down but also right and left, so that there is no position to enter that circle that he draws with that dagger that looks more like a bayonet, and I don't know what I am going to do because I have nothing loaded in my hand at the time and the knife I took is short and so I am just scrubbing up dirt with my hand and I consider throwing some of it down his throat, and at this very moment I see a rock looking like a big cobblestone and I grab this rock and with an anger I cannot describe, because the thing was cutting my hand, I look straight at the root of his nose, I take a good look at his face and let the rock go on his face with all the might I can gather and I see him founder right away and the blood spurt. Yes, you are going to take it, yes, you are, take it, take it, take it! I push it in, you bad pox, I almost can't hold the rock up any longer. I was lying belly down and I had gotten there crawling and my soul was coming out through my lungs, but I still held it up with both hands, aimed slowly and pounded on his face with the rock once more with both hands. I heard only the sound of his face caving in, tchunk, like a broken watermelon, and his blood ran down inside my sleeve and the stone rolled and fell in his lap and stopped.

Well, I had never really done that, I only knew about it from hearsay, but I suddenly felt like it, so that I sat there for a while seeing the dagger, which was lying motionless on the ground. And then I dragged him inside through the gate. A visitor, a visitor, Sr. Nestor, a visitor with a warped face. 67

Master of the house
Open this door
There is a visitor
With a warped face.

And I went on singing low and dragging him by the hair, and I got to the gate and with the same dagger he had been scratching the air with, with that very same dagger he had been swishing, I cut his neck back and forth, it being easier than I had thought before trying, with that very same dagger he had on his hip and later fenced with calling me a cuckold, I cut his neck, it was really much, much easier than I had expected and inside there were many more things than I had expected too, a lot of sinews, and only the bone in the back took a little longer, but I found a gap between two little bones, exactly like an oxtail, and then it became easy, the marrow being quickly sliced to end things, God's cavalry for justice, go call your father a cuckold, and there was blood like from four faucets to a distance greater than you would suppose, but soon it ran out and trickled down and stopped for good. From which it is evident that a man squirts blood farther than he can spit.

I've had better dreams, because today's dreams are about a wonderment of frogs. Big frogs with mouths even bigger that stand at attention in front of me. It's impossible to cut off a frog's head without cutting the whole rest of the body for lack of a neck, but as for the lieutenant, as soon as I had finished the beheading I was able to tie his head to the end of a piece of rope and swirl it around my own head and march downward, and I still don't know how I didn't die because they didn't stop, but I remained there for some time facing them and saying, "Look at his head, look at his head, whoever persists will end up like this too," and then I jerked the rope and threw the head in the middle of the force, which stopped for a while since the head was an ugly thing, a twisted thing, in view of the fact that he didn't close his eyes well and the color was the ugliest and there was still dirt even inside the ears and besides I had smashed the front parts before, so that it was a horror and it must have impaired the force of the force. But I could not stay there, having the responsibility of taking the creature with me, which is the reason why we are here and we are not going to stay here, moreover this is a very crazy priest. I dream of a pile of frogs, or it's not a dream, I don't know, Amaro sleeps and the creature is in vigil, I guarantee it. Well, there are these frogs. One of the frogs is called Natércio and he'd rather laugh than do anything else. A frog laughs with his arms crossed. And he stays there, thinking of flies, fireflies and beetles. The other frog, whose name is Roque Pedrosa, is more serious and only laughs now and then, when he sees the need for it. Whenever he thinks the need arises for him to laugh he stops and does some thinking, some hard thinking, and then he asks: In this case, my dear friend, you think there is a need for a laugh? If the dear friend says yes, he asks: Do you guarantee it? If he guarantees it, then he laughs, but in a very polite way, with his hand over his mouth and without making too much noise. There is another frog, by the name of Esteves Jaques, who is a graduated frog and who looks very important and gives advice to others and makes a lot of propaganda, but is no good because he likes only money and brandy and looking like a saint and who gives a damn about other people's troubles? It is such a long line of frogs you have to see it to believe it. You could put these frogs through a close order drill, except that Esteves Jaques keeps causing a great deal of confusion, saying bad things about his friends to his wife and saying he's the only good one, without a fault, and telling his wife everything his friends tell him and meanwhile he's crossing himself very grandly, until a tre- *69* mendous quarrel breaks out, everything sounding like a drum corps with all those frog mouths clapping. All of them are toothless, but have plenty of echo inside. Also, I suffer memories, like when I ate in São Cristóvão at the home of a National Democrat who lives there, a very rich man who however is a National Democrat and a friend of the boss, I don't know how, and he likes to laugh like that frog Natércio. They even look alike, only the frog doesn't have a mustache so the likeness is not so much. First: The table the likes of which I have never seen, of dark wood, maybe from an ashleaf startree, very impressive, on a porch, half a porch, a piece of it outside the house, a piece inside, a few trees, cajarana, oiti, avocado, this one very large, and some more deep into the back yard. You should have seen what a breeze was blowing, a genuinely cool breeze, which made a man think of two hammock hooks there to sleep or to stretch out, a quiet and cool town making a noise like rain on leaves and out there was a sun, but a sun that just slipped downhill without hurting, touching the smooth stones and glittering, turning by the church and finishing below, on a square they have in São Cristóvão from which you can see the church and from the church you can see it, as if they had the sea over there, because everything is blue above the church, and there are some old streets that run like rivers and people know they are old because they are crooked and have no width, and the houses standing right across each other from huge window to huge window with so many parts to open, and the sun comes back uphill and goes on like that, and from inside you can sit down and stretch out your hand to break chayote tendrils between your fingers or to try to uncurl them, they look like springs and one pulls and pulls without paying too much attention and forgetting about life, or then remembering a real life, sitting, feeling. Second: The food. The man said: "Today we are gathered together here in order to eat, thanks be to God, therefore let us eat, thanks be to God," and he crossed himself, he acted like a Protestant. Since Protestants have dealings with the devil, I became suspicious, and besides he was a National Democrat. But he was no Protestant because he did not sing, like the Protestants I helped stone in Aracaju with all their singing and something written on the wall of their place: If you come in peace you may come in, but show respect for other people's religions, and we threw stones just the same, why not, because Protestants don't dance, don't play, don't piss and when they die they don't rot away, they keep on suffering. Nevertheless, he was not a Protestant. Well, we are here to eat, thanks be to God, and let us everybody eat, without hurrying. Whoever has something to do don't do it here, because at the strike of one we start to eat, after these gold-waters, these vermouths, these firewaters, after these pop-skulls, these rotguts, these liquid fires, after these tonics, no matter what time it is we only stop eating when we feel like it, thanks be to God, and we can eat as much as we care to, thanks be to God, that's what food is for, isn't it? There were four maids, two of them wearing hats and white aprons and holding trays you had to use both hands to carry, for they were filled to the brim. Third: The food itself, of which the first to come were fish-farm mullet, fat and oily. There were two types, some broiled in leaves and the leaves were glossy and it is necessary to turn them over so as not to miss the fat, and the smell, the meat came off the bones easily, ah. One could dive into that white manioc mush and there was a hot sauce of the cooked kind inside it, an oil upon which whole peppers were floating, the sort that swell up and get dark, with bubbles, among green spices; it was good to look at the sauce and stir it slowly with the spoon. The other kind of mullet was a stew in dende oil with yellow manioc mush and this one had fish slices inside the tureen, some parts of the slices were darker than others and some were softer and one could pick the tail part and go about taking off the meat with care so as to leave only the bone and the tail end. It was easily boned and more gravy was poured on the mush and each piece was better than the one before. On the side: Crayfish, some quartered and in a dende stew, and the others fried as they came from the river in saltless butter but with salt on the crayfish, in the white butter, a smell good to smell. Best of all, the little crayfish that don't even have a complete shell and that we ate one by one looking at the next one in order to be able to make a good choice. Before that, large oysters, big as biscuits, and these can either be had raw or boiled, the raw ones being preferable because they don't require you to drop them on a plate like a steak but can be eaten from the shell with a noise, a mussel loaf in a bowl which you can mix with the gravy and throw on the oysters, and some fried land crab without the shells, and meanwhile we are sprinkling a little bit of yellow rock salt on the oysters, all the color of egg yellows and gold, and the hot sauce stifling us, it is good because it gives you a very good virility. We ate several foods, and there were more, only we didn't eat them. And I am eating and looking at the other stuff all the time. The man of the house said, afterward everybody can sleep in a hammock if there are enough hammocks. Fourth: Beans and kale in which we put manioc flour and mix and mix and place on top of it minced fried jerked beef and add some sweet mango and some watermelon. There was pork from a sow they had killed just before, a thin and fatless little pig with almost no bones, only those that had to remain as a matter of taste, and this pork also went its way. And there was a big piece of sun-dried meat which was eaten last of all, because the man said, after sun-dried meat everything becomes tasteless, you have to leave it for last, and it is true. This one

72 you can even eat raw, like ham. But it was not raw, it was

broiled. A big piece of sun-dried meat, fat on one side and lean on the other, it went its way too, on top of milk-and-manioc-flour mush, made just right, not lumpy, not thin, ah. The meat was cut in front of everybody, all of us waiting and watching, and nothing was denied, a two-pronged fork lifting it and a swift knife cutting out slices and dropping them on top of the mush with gravy. In the middle, here and there, a few little pieces of onion, almost unrecognizable, charred and black but giving out much happiness to the gravy. The gravy was a slow gravy, and thick, flowing, flowing, ah. Everybody silent, eating silently and burping. When someone had to burp he looked the other way and unfastened his belt and leaned back and sometimes there were stops for sighing, everybody uncinched and wide and looking up without seeing anything and picking out a little something from between their teeth. In silence, ah. Fifth: A cashew fruit compote of which the syrup looked like wine with cashew fruits in it and the cashew fruits looked like they were handmade that way on purpose, and then one breaks the goat cheese which is tangy and has a smell that doesn't lie to anybody, and first one puts the cheese on the plate and the cashew fruits on top, with a lot of syrup. And one eats the cashew fruits. We ate the cashew fruits and the host took to eating pitombas and spitting the seeds on the back yard. "This land is so good," the man said, "that all of these seeds sprout later on and the place is filled with pitomba trees." I caressed a few more cashew fruits. "And I have good blood," the host said. "It is enough to spit out a few seeds or to throw them around like marbles for them to sprout," and we started a sluggish conversation while the coffee was being ground, and the coffee came and we remained. The host said, "Thanks be to God," and then we slept in the hammocks, and there were no dreams.

Now this priest, when everybody woke up and I was by   73

the window looking at the street through the shutters and feeling a giddiness I always feel when I smoke my first cigarette in the morning and listening to the sound of corn being grated for the morning meal, this priest comes in and tells us to wait, because we are supposed to wait for the answer to the message he sent a few people, or then we have to march on to Flower Island or something, and then the priest gets his dander up and says a lot of bad words and says no one is going to leave the place at all until the people who are to decide on the matter arrive. "Because this matter is already smelling rotten," the priest says, "and I don't even know which of the following things you should do: Either you put this Christian to an end directly, praise Our Lord Jesus Christ, Our Lord Jesus Christ be praised, or then you turn him loose," the priest says, "because I don't know if it's still possible to take him to the capital, and that's the truth. Especially because," the priest says, "we have atrocity here, extracted teeth, violences, and times are changing and you cut off a lieutenant's head and I don't know what's going to happen, if only he were a corporal or something like that, but how can anyone cut off an officer's head even in the heat of battle, I think it's madness. To belt him a few times, all right, to pull out one of his eyes in the struggle or something like that, which you almost don't do on purpose, these things will happen. But not cutting a head off. When you cut a head off you have to look at the neck and to make up your mind about cutting, it's a cold decision, unacceptable." But at this moment he sits on the settee and looks at the creature and looks more and more and then he calms down.

"That's the way it is. There are many heads in this God's world."

"The lieutenant called me a cuckold, Sr. Priest. It was he or I."

"That's the way it is," the priest says. "You did the right thing."

And he crossed himself and said he didn't have to say that. "The thing is that the situation has changed," the priest says. "I don't know whether you will be able to take the man to Aracaju, because there are more people there than ever before and also newspapers and they say that when you get there they will fill your hide with lead and turn the man loose. I don't believe Antunes will be able to support you." "Ah, no, not that, if Antunes can't support me, what can?" "I don't know, the priest said, and stuck his hands in his frock with his legs spread out and sat there with his head hanging. "This land," he says after a long time, "was a good land once because there were more real men and whoever was a real man had nothing to fear. Today this land is not worth anything anymore, almost not worth anything. It's covered with yellowness and a man doesn't know what he can depend upon and they want to change everything and it's never going to work. Because if they take away a man's resources, what do they leave him? Nothing. A life, maybe, but this is not a man's life, it's a funeral. I don't know, I don't know," the priest says, shaking his head and pursing his lips. "Why don't you disappear?" "Me disappear, me disappear? How can I disappear if first I am myself and see myself all the time, I can't disappear from myself and when I am there I am always there, I can never disappear. Other people can disappear, not ourselves." "Well, that's true," the priest says. "The others are the ones who can always disappear, never ourselves."

"Ahn-well, besides, I'm not sure there are many men in Aracaju who can stop me like that. Besides, the chief told me to go look for this creature and I went, I caught him, brought him along, broke him and I am going to take him, even if the 75 chief can no longer support me I will have taken the man and delivered him. It is necessary to deliver the animal. I deliver him and I say: Mission accomplished. After that, they can take care of the rest the best they can, but the delivery will have been made, I am not the kind of man to stop halfway. If things are really the way they say they are I am going to wait for new orders, because this one has been given, and even if he came over here and asked me not to take him I would not accept that, because maybe he is just trying to help me stay out of trouble and I am not afraid of trouble, I will take this trash with me no matter what, I will get there and deliver him. Even if I burst. I want to see who is man enough in Aracaju to tell me I can't do it, because I am Getúlio Santos Bezerra and my equal has not yet been born. I am Getúlio Santos Bezerra and my name is a verse and my grandfather was tough and everybody in my stock is tough and my mother was called Justa and was tough and in these backlands no one is tougher than I, in everything I am better. Try me. Getúlio Santos Bezerra I am called, and while you kill a sheep by giving a blow to his head with a mortar, I can kill the same sheep or any other with a punch to its head and I can kill any living being and I can handle well these irons I carry. I run, I roar and I shoot better and wound better and drink better and fight better and strike better and have four-teen bullets in my body and cut heads off and kill anything and nothing kills me. And I am not afraid of ghosts, I am not afraid of bogeymen, I am not afraid of werewolves, I am not afraid of darkness, I am not afraid of Hell, I am not afraid of any goddamned big or little thing. And I don't listen to harsh words, I don't make empty threats, I don't say bad things about my women, I don't owe any favors and I don't like to be touched. You have heard my name, Getúlio Santos Bezerra, it is I, and when I laugh everyone can start trembling and when I frown everybody can start trembling and if I stomp my foot on the ground everybody can start running and if I blow on anybody's face you can deliver your soul unto God. Snakes don't do me any harm and I can stand hunger, I can stand cold, I can stand anything and if they cut me up I won't flinch. I can sleep on the floor, I can sleep on twigs, I can sleep on leather and I can do without sleeping and the first one who shows his face will see me shoot first and when I shoot I don't shoot at the legs, rather I shoot at the face or I shoot at the chest and the holes I carve are sometimes one on top of the other and heed this: All of Sergipe can't boast of anyone better than I and if I tell you that no one is better than I in Sergipe, I am telling you that no one is better in the whole world, because this is a man's land and I am the man of this land. If I am supposed to wait, I will wait, but waiting is not the same as stopping. And I am going to drag this junk over to Aracaju if I have to impale him, we will ride in that Hudson to Aracaju, and when we get there we will present him: He came from Paulo Afonso to here and his mouth is in poor shape because it got termites on the way and they ate up his front teeth. And if I cut off the lieutenant's head, it was well done. But I am not going to tell everybody that I cut off the lieutenant's head. I will tell only the chief and then I will shut my mouth and cross my arms and set my eyes on the wind. And set your eyes upon mine if you dare. And that's it. And if nobody wants to go along with me I am going all by myself, you hear that Amaro?" "Yes," the priest said, "I am not that much of a man."

V

I can't say I like being here on the second floor of the priest's house without doing anything and every day hearing the bell toll starting early in the morning and having no will even to shave. The priest comes over and tells a few stories. He also brought a set of dominoes which I play with Amaro until we get bored, then we play checkers and we get bored too and stop again. I called the priest and told him, I will wait until tomorrow. If no one has come by tomorrow I am going to hit the road, no one can restrain me. Amaro says that if he repeats every move I make with my checker pieces I will be given a full block, I will get all stuck. We examine this, starting from the corners, which is the best way. It's a fact, if you don't take any pieces, it all gets stuck. I will never figure that out. I have no patience to keep studying these pieces on this board, it heats up one's head, it has no purpose. Not Amaro, he keeps on talking about checkers as if it amounted to something. Also, I don't play without panting and Amaro plays without panting. I don't understand this. It's better when you pant, it's more fun. Son of his mother, he plays checkers like a sprinting gamecock. He yields and yields and then whop! — the betrayal. He blocks you and says the blocking of one piece is worth twenty-five points, and a three-piece block is worth thirty points, I've never heard of these rules. Same thing with dominoes, a lot of ideas about doubles, each one worth this or that. This is impossible, I don't believe in this kind of game. I could try to return to Nestor's ranch, but I might be disappointed, there is a war there, with complete certainty. It was better over there, at least there were the cattle and the frogs for us to say nasty things about, and Amaro could go on cutting his razor sedge stalks without doing any annoying. Over here he is always after me, he needs company, the pest. Now and then I peek through the shutters and there are some boys flying kites, for it is September and kite-flying time more or less, just like there is a time for tops and a time for jacks and a time for marbles. I don't know how these times arise, but there is a time for everything. Silly little kites with nothing on them, well you probably can't find even string in this town. I myself could never fly a kite, couldn't do it right, but I enjoyed splitting up other people's tops and did not enjoy people splitting up mine. Skinny boys who never saw any other place and then they go away and disappear and only the spinsters remain, without men. The fellow goes to live in Aracaju and says, I was born in Japoatão. Well, what do you know! And they keep on being born, there are more people being born each day. There are people being born even in Muribeca, huh Amaro? Ahn-well. This priest is too nervous, what he needs is a couple of nuns here for him to screw. You think the priest screws nuns, Amaro? It may well be that nothing happens, some people say it is like that. He sings: 79

Captain Moreira César
Eight and ten wars he won
He couldn't finish his third
He died on Belo Monte.

A deep voice, and he claps his hands while he sings:

Ensign Vanderlei
Is more than opinionated
When he went to Canudo for the war
He rode out in front of the batallion.

The buzzards of Canudo
Have written to the President
That their bills are wearing thin
From eating so many people.

The buzzards of Canudo
Have written to the capital
That their bills are wearing thin
From eating so many officers.

Ensign Joaquim Teles
May be one of the toughest
When he went to Canudo
He stayed in the sick ward.

The government weaknesses
Went through Cocorobó
After they passed through there
Only the government remained.

Ensign Luiz Peçanha
Was a very brave man
When he got to Canudo
He was attacked by toothache.

Ensign Martim Francisco
Wanted to win the war
When he got to Canudo
He was buried in the ground.

Ensign Manuel da Costa
Was very mean and tough
When he got to Canudo
He ran away to Japoatão.

This he sings without changing his voice and he breaks the music with jokes, like the time he came up here and explained how many people had died in Canudo and how they stuffed nails into their shotguns to use them as bullets. One picked a nail, the priest said, a rusty nail, and after stuffing plenty of gunpowder down the barrel you rammed in the nail, and a nail such as that, all loose inside the barrel, made a tremendous damage in the recipient, so that when he did not die of the nailing he died of the disease given by the rust of the nail. Which means many good men were nailed to death over there.

"The mortality was so high," the priest said, "that the buzzards would eat only commanding officers."

And he laughed and went downstairs. And then I stay here like a cow, I stay like I don't know what, waiting for those people to bring me a decision for me to move somewhere, I really can't endure it any longer. Well, tomorrow I will let myself loose in the world, there is no way I will stay. Whence come those men, upon what nags will they be riding, what sensitivities will they show? I don't understand it well. The priest also comes to teach me a couple of prayers, and Amaro and I apply ourselves to learning the prayers and the creature sometimes tries to intrude. The first time I resolved to gag him once more because I feared he would shout for assist- 81 ance, but the priest said he could shout as much as he felt like since there was no way for anyone to hear him. But I told him anyway, I told him very clearly, I said: "Look, pox, if you shout I will have the bell rung so that your noise will not be heard, I am going to make them ring out a happy toll and in the same beat as the toll I will finish the rest of your teeth, so you will stop being a fool. And you accomplish nothing by looking at the priest because I'm already furious, stuck in this hole, and if you think you are safe because of all this talk you have been hearing about setting you free, I will have you know, senhor, that your fate is written and you are going with me to Aracaju for me to deliver you and lock you up in a dump in which you will suffer some two dozen backfuckings, since the other prisoners are always horny, you understand. You have seen how I chopped the lieutenant's head off and would not give a second thought to chopping off the head of whoever appears, stripes or no stripes, including your head, at least I would have something to do, because I would trim it here, trim it there and would make a little football and would kick it around with Amaro, or else I would give it to those kids for a soccer game down there." The priest says, "What are you saying, Sergeant, are we losing our tempers here," and I say, "That's right, Priest, that's right," and this creature is already making me so edgy I can't endure it, I have never been so disturbed, I don't like him. It's as though I felt like crying, but out of pity for myself. I keep thinking up things to do to him. To put a zipper on his mouth with a padlock, open it, throw an ember in and close it and watch it smoke. I'll tell you, a person can go crazy on an inconclusive mission such as this, and all these mysteriousnesses, you can't do this and you can't do that, why can't I? Why can't I, why can't I? You can't do anything, there is always somebody to inform you that you can't. Well, you can. What is there that I can't do, I ask you this, why shit. But now and then the priest gives me a reprimand, such thick reprimands that I have to shut my mouth, because the priest also carries that dangerous double barrel to and fro and he looks like if he aims he will shoot and I do not wish to kill a priest, it sets you back. But it is because in these hours when you have nothing to do, in these hours an itching comes over me to torment the creature and the more he stands still the more I feel like tormenting and pulling and hitting, that's how it is. Now the priest comes over and teaches the prayers and crosses himself and kneels down, so we also kneel down and pray and the thing is the one who prays the most and all the time we are praying I feel like tormenting him, give me your hand so I can blow my nose in it, I don't want to mess mine up, but I say nothing and we remain there looking upward and calling out a couple of prayers. The truth is the creature has the greatest need for prayers, because he probably is not very happy with the way his life has been going lately, because he doesn't look well, he is thinner and feeble and no longer wishes to shave. The gums healed well and have started to shrink, the other day I pulled up his lips and looked. The lack of teeth does not suit him well, the mouth looks like an inverted flower. It is a perfect asshole mouth and when speech comes out, it comes out among whistles. It's interesting. Also he hasn't washed, he must be full of nits in his beard and he stinks plentifully. Well, everyone lives the way he chooses.

In any case, I repeat to the priest, in any case I will stay here no longer, and I say that to Amaro too, who said that with the Hudson hidden away with no chance to be warmed up he can't promise anything, and that he doesn't know if the gas in the cans in the back is drying up, and that in this land you can't buy even a coin's worth of gasoline, and a lot of sniveling. Amaro has always been like this. It doesn't matter, if that contraption breaks down we leave it on the   83 road and we go on walking, it might even be better. Because cars have no shoes we can wear backward, so followers think we are going the other way, isn't that right? We are going anyway, I don't think there is anybody following us, just because I don't believe Nestor is going to say who cut the lieutenant's head off, I don't even believe anybody is still alive out there. I don't know, I don't know anything, but I won't stay here anymore and I am going to leave first thing in the morning tomorrow before sunup. But the priest comes over and tells me I can't go tomorrow because he got a message saying that the men will come tomorrow for a talk, so it is suitable to stay. Ahn-well, I will stay but only until tomorrow and then I will leave. I don't know how to talk well anyway and I owe explanations to only one person, thank God, and I have heard nothing from that person as yet, except what people keep telling me, only you can't impress me through my ears. I have to see it, that's the way it is. Priest, what men might those be? I don't know, the priest says, they are influential, I think. They are influential. Well, first is God who art in Heaven. Second, I don't know. When I was a young man, it was the owner of a cotton machine. When I was very little, it was the owner of a sugar cane machine. I don't really know, these things are confusing. The priest said, "You had no business cutting off the lieutenant's head, now you are a deserter and there isn't much that can be done for you." Now, this is all very strange, I never saw so much nonsense on account of a shitty lieutenant's head. Not even if he was high-ranking, no one has any more respect for stripes these days. It happened, it happened, that's all. One must be a man, it happened and that's it. The lieutenant is up in Heaven, Sr. Priest, all right, he must be wearing wings and playing the guitar and better off than the rest of us down here. Maybe it is the priest, he seems to be an important priest. Maybe it is all the priests, after God. I don't know. There are the candidates for the presidency, Cristiano Machado and the brigadier and Getúlio Vargas. The governor. No, there also are the friends. I don't know how all this is arranged. I wish I knew a little, maybe Amaro knows but I am not going to ask him because I don't want to appear ignorant. Forget it, if I were to think I would not understand; in effect the world is like this, it is the chief and it is I. I mean, there are other people, but they are not people for me, because they are outside. I don't know. Ahn. I mean, I am here. I am I. If I want to be I the right way, it has to be with the chief because otherwise I would be something else, but I am I and I can't be anything else. I am getting old, I must be over thirty. I must be over forty, maybe, and I have been noticing white hairs in my beard for some time. I can't be anything else, and that means I have to do well the things I do, because if I don't how is it going to turn out? What will I be? I don't like this talk about men coming here to talk. If the chief comes, all right. If he doesn't come, I don't know. I am a sergeant in the military militia of the state of Sergipe. I am nothing, I am Getúlio. I really would like to see the chief now because I get tired alone, I have to think, I don't understand things well. I am a sergeant in the military militia of the state of Sergipe. What is that? I stare at this fold in the cloth of my uniform which rubs my chin. I am nothing, that's what. I like to eat, to sleep and to do things. I don't like what I don't understand, I get tired. If I got there I would sit down, tell my story and await a decision. It would be much better. The way it is, I don't know. I don't like the world to change, it gives me an uneasy feeling, I don't know what to do. That is why the only thing I can do is to take this trash to Aracaju and deliver it. It has to be. Then I will decide about the other things and so forth. I don't know if these people are from the Yellow Boot Syndicate, if they want to get me, if they can be trusted. Those yellow-booters do their job quickly. The 85 man is sitting by his door in his pajamas and his repose, sitting in a wicker chair, and the gunman comes along — good evening, pardon my imposing on you, what time might it be? And then from under his armpit, through the coat, looking the other way, he plugs the man twice and walks away just the way he came. I don't like them, they receive money to do that, I don't think it is right. In any case when the men arrive, friend or no friend, I will slip my hand under the table holding something pointed the way of their chins from underneath. If I have to go I will not go alone, and I don't feel like going now. I have to warn Amaro. It may be a fusillade. I wonder if the priest will let me borrow that two-barreled one.

That big bald one, that one I saw once when they killed Arnaldo at the Christmas fair and we had a great hubbub and he was in the middle of the confusion in the police station saying that he just lifted his beer glass and when he raised his beer glass there were only two shots one on top of the other. They are going to say it was Mário Barreto, they are going to say it was Mário Barreto. I am here knowing it wasn't Mário Barreto, in fact I know exactly who did it but I don't feel like saying it because I am not supposed to say it anyway. I stay silent looking at him. He likes to rub his hands together and has a golden tooth, I mean, half a golden tooth, which glitters. I don't know the other two, never saw them before. There is one who wears sandals, talks in splutters and has a mustache. I don't like this one's face, as his eyes never stop. This other one is the one I am going to point the iron at, he doesn't say anything and is thick around the ribs, there must be artillery there. It may be that it may be meant for me, it may not be, he had better not scratch himself, it would be better, because if he scratches himself from this very table where I am now — and I am very well at this table, with my legs stretched and my feet on a chair and I

86

don't seem to be up to anything, even thinking about life, I am rubbing my belly like this with one hand and holding the old warrior under my jacket looking the other way, and if you just glance at me I would seem to you to be without a care, and I don't set my eyes on the silent one since it is he I am going to shoot first if necessary, and there is nothing in my appearance and I even feel like having a couple of drinks, like laughing a little, it is a cool day, a good day, and one would think there is nothing in the air, but from this very place where I am just by moving my forefinger with this expressionless face I can blow a hole through this table here straight toward that one's jaw. It seems I prefer thinking about shooting him to listening to the conversation. That's all right, his blood does not agree with my blood. It would rip through my jacket but that's not a problem, I would fix it. Well, the bald one does the talking, but the one with the mustache wants to talk too and he can't very well do it, he chokes on his speech, how could a thing like that ever get a diploma. By now, I say, by now all of Sergipe already knows that the gentlemen are here and that I am here. And I am already guessing what the bald one is going to answer. It bothers me to see the one with the mustache wiggling all over his chair. I feel like telling him to cut that out, but I can't do it, I have to know my place. You, Sergeant, you killed the lieutenant and destroyed the patrol. Hum-hum, hum-hum. You cut the lieutenant's head off and whirled it at the end of a rope. Chatter-chatter. We don't live by the law of the jungle. A fine thing to do. You, Sergeant, you did a lot of things. Chatter-chatter. I'm listening, it sounds like my mother speaking, when she spoke. I did what I had to do, being a lieutenant does not give him the right to call me a cuckold; besides, it was he or I. Besides, I didn't cut his head off, a man did it. What man? Now, that I don't remember, there was much dust, it was difficult for anybody to see his   87 own feet. I was never one to kill anyone that way, it was a cheap man, whoever heard of cutting off a lieutenant's head on Friday, it is not done. Hum. I have to sneak an eye at the silent one who may be moving, but he has both hands on the table, and he'd better. The mad one rose. "Sergeant, look, Sergeant, the problem is that it was a mistake, Sergeant, a mistake to send you to get a man in Paulo Afonso, now we have complications." "Who said that, the chief?" "It was the chief who said it, there are no more conditions for coverage, things have changed." "Did the chief send this message?" "Yes, yes." "And why didn't he come himself? Now, answer this one." "He didn't come because he doesn't want to let anybody know he is behind all of it. There are federal forces coming, there is everything. Therefore you set the man free and disappear and that's all. And the rest will be taken care of in Aracaju."

"I can't disappear. Only other people can disappear. How can I disappear, if I am I? Besides, if you gentlemen want me to set the man free and disappear, that's because later on he and yourselves will come after me, to pull me out of Hell itself so as to make me take the blame."

"You have my word of honor."

"You can keep your word for yourself, all I have is what is mine, little as it is. I will do as follows: What follows is as follows: I will decide about this today. You gentlemen leave, I stay and talk to the priest and then set the man free. But with you here I won't do that, I need guarantees." The silent one moved, and I said, "My good friend I have noticed that you carry an armament under there, but do me the favor of allowing me to tell you a little thing, one little, tiny thing: In the first place I have never feared any man and I have seen several bigger than you, but for all of them a little bullet of the same size is sufficient, it's enough for it to be well placed. In the second place, do me the favor of noticing that this hand of mine which is down here is not scratching my private parts but is resting on a Smith, believe me, a fine Smith as good as can be, and if you insist I will show it to you, senhor. In the third place, Amaro is over there with something behind him, right over the church's balustrade, aren't you Amaro, huh Amaro? You need not look behind you, that thing is a beauty, he borrowed it from a friend of mine, he likes it very much, don't you, Amaro? Believe me he likes it and have you ever seen how a trigger of that sort is soft to pull because it has a spring, and this spring needs only the rubbing of a finger to come loose and when it comes loose it makes the hammers hit the caps and when the caps are hit they explode and when they explode they spread this dreadfully hot lead, all you have to do is ask." "Sergeant, let's calm down, chatter-chatter." "But I am calm. You told me that the chief no longer wants to have anything to do with this, I believe, I believe. Things being this way, I can set the man free but not as long as you gentlemen are here, so that I expect you gentlemen to be leaving as peacefully as you have arrived, and after you gentlemen leave I will set the man free and go away."

I don't even know how I could speak like that, but suddenly I was feeling very well and what else can happen to me. What can happen to me is dying and after that there is nothing else, and if I die I will take several people with me, it is going to be a caravan, and when the men desisted from doing any more talking and when I remembered Elevaldo's message and when I saw they had gone away and I had to make a decision, then I don't know. I don't like all this message fuss, it is not my way. But maybe everything is true, and then I am alone in the world, I together with Amaro. Now see, I can't answer for Amaro, I can answer for myself. What did he say to me? He said to me, bring that man here at least half whole. He is going with only four teeth missing, 89 he can get replacements afterward, and also missing a little fat, which is a good thing on account of the heat. Now, if I heed the message and don't take the man back I will be in an awkward position, and maybe the message isn't even true. If I take him back, at least I will see it with my own eyes, and dying one way or another is the same thing. But the chief may not like it. I don't know. I don't like this.

I take him back or I don't take him back, that's the question. Maybe it's better to suffer one's luck no matter what it is, for it must have been written so. Or it's better to fight everything and finish everything. To die is like sleeping and to sleep is to put an end to agony, which is why we always want to sleep. It's just that sleeping can bring you dreams and then everything stays the same. For this reason it's better to die, because there are no dreams when you turn your soul loose and everything ends. Because life is too long and has disasters. Why endure old age coming slowly, tyrannifications and false orders, the pain of cuckoldry, the slowness of things, the things that can't be understood, and the ungratefulness that's undeserved, if you can dispatch yourself with a plain knife? Who can carry this weight, in this life that brings only sweat and fights? The ones who endure it are those who are afraid of death because no one has ever come back from there, and this is what weakens the wish to die. And then you go on putting up with bad things so as not to have to try others that we still don't know. And it is by thinking that you become yellow and the will to fight fades when you think about it and when you remember this you forget about what you were going to do and end up not doing anything at all. Priest, most reverend, in your prayers remember my sins.

I am going to do as follows, I am going to take him, yes. I was never a man to fail halfway, yes, I will take him. I know that you, Sr. Priest, prefer that I leave this junk here but I will not do that, and you can say I said it and you can say that I even disobeyed orders violently, but I am going to take the man with me even if I have to leave pieces of him along the way, anything. I can head anywhere anyway, I can go and come back, I can make labyrinthicals: I step out of here, circle around Muribeca, go up to Malhada dos Bois, strike out for Gararu, return to Amparode São Francisco, slide to Aquidabã and Cumbe, throw myself to Feira Nova and Divina Pastora and Santa Rosa de Lima and Malhador and Rosário do Catete and Maruim and I go into Santo Amaro das Brotas and hurl myself downriver and there is no one to catch me, no one has ever seen a sergeant in a canoe or whatever and I stop at Barra dos Coqueiros and there is no one to hold me, I arrive there and arrange things and put an end to all this situation and in all those places no mayor nor marshal nor deputy can lay their hands on me, and some of the places have no marshal or mayor, they are not even towns, so I am going. Look, if a saint asked me, do you wish to die old and cowardly or do you wish to die at this age and valiant, I can assure you I would say I would want to die a man, I see nothing in any other way. And besides this is already getting on my nerves and I want to stop. And besides I don't want to live hiding around or to go and be a driver in São Paulo, I don't even know where that is, so if I may just stick my hand in that holy water bowl and cross myself and pack up my things. I think so much irritation is giving me a fever, I get like this once in a while, I can't endure it, period. God keep me from not taking back the thing with me and not delivering him, what am I going to think afterward, since I have but little to think about and the little I have keeps swelling in my head and taking over the hollow inside? I thank you for the food and the rest and the singing and the talks and the trouble you took for us. And I would appreciate it if we could borrow, and it may never return, this little thing that Amaro likes so   91 much and gets along so well with and it breaks his heart to leave it, I know that you can get one like it where you got it, a priest such as you. I come in through one door, I go out through the same door, may you have a good day.

VI

All houses look like platefuls of food even if it is manioc
flour mush. This Hudson, when it broke down for lack of
gasoline, I gave it a good look and thought it was quite a
monarch of a thing, because it necessitated the putting of
gasoline in it by us and we used up all the cans and I wonder
where the hell we are in this world. To tell the truth, I do
know, but I see that walking is the thing that must be done
and the junk opens his mouth and says that he cannot walk.
And I say, yes, you can walk. Otherwise I will do the worst
things to you, don't get fresh. But I really wouldn't do anything, with all this tiredness and even my jacket I took off
because it weighed on me, I can barely carry my weapon and
Amaro his, he actually likes it very much, he does everything
short of kissing it, in fact I think he does, at night when no
one is watching he gives it a few kisses. I know he polishes
it with the cloth he got from the car. I stood looking at this
car, which is new but has long become old, and I remained
looking at it, all cold. It stood there, dead. Amaro still lifted
the hood and looked inside, a heap of parts it had inside, all
still; even Hudsons die. Then what is left for Amaro is the

little two-barreled thing, which he strokes and polishes and sniffs and when he leans it against something he pulls back and makes it stand on its butt and takes to gazing at it like a father gazes at a daughter. This Amaro is my brother, because there is only him in the world now, I can believe that, he is the only one in the world who doesn't think I am touched in the head, and the truth is I really am a little disturbed in the mind, with all those leagues I have swallowed and harnessed to this pox besides, the only word for it is harnessed for he is always hanging from me and drags himself along, he is really excessively weak, the only politics he is fit for is verbal politics. Then I tell him: I will do the worst things to you, you hear? He doesn't even answer, this one also thinks I am unbalanced, let him think. Well then: I will hang your head down from a tree and stick your head into a barrel full of fine sand like the one from Sand Hill in Aracaju, a very fine sand you can't even hold in your hands, and will leave you there taking breaths of sand. You breathe, you breathe and you fill your bellows with sand and it hurts so that I can't even tell you, hah. He doesn't believe me anymore, I guess. Or then he believes but it doesn't reach him anymore, perhaps he no longer remembers his own name. Nobody remembers his name any longer, nobody remembers even our names, I mean, I remember my name and Amaro's name and if I wanted to I could remember the creature's name, but I don't want to and I forgot it. And that's that. And then we go on like that and every now and then he balks like a mule and we have to spur him so he will proceed. Sometimes I do the spurring, sometimes Amaro does it, but I prefer doing it myself, because Amaro doesn't spur well. He spurs badly. When he pushes the spur against the thing's sides he makes a grimace and holds his hand back a little. There are a few things missing in Amaro, I don't

94 know what it is; if he doesn't change someone will get him,

I always say. Well, I take the spur from him and show him how it is done — it's like this, hey, hum! — but he is hopeless for when he uses the spur it is with the same wavering and a funny face wrinkling his eyes. We have to spur this prisoner or he won't walk, it's not just, one should not delay people like this, but I can see that the way he has been going one of these days he won't even pay any attention to the spur, no doubt his ass is one whole callus now, but I will sharpen this spur very well someday and I want to see him walk at least until we run into a place where we can rest our backs a little and get back on the road again. I know there are people after us, one can smell a certain stench if one looks backward, but I don't want any combats because the devil may interfere and then I won't be able to get to Aracaju with the pox at my side, and that is something I am going to do, I will drag him to Aracaju if I have to, if I have to, I don't know how, but I will drag him. This poor devil of an old machine-gunned Hudson, with a door you can say it was welded by machine-gun fire, it has seen many things. These holes look like rivet holes, they look like pan plugs. It has seen many things. Ahn-well, there it stays with its hood raised like a dead burro and after a long time somebody finds it with hornets building their nests on its parts and game birds scurrying under it. It turns into a statue. Forget it.

Well, you walk, pox, or I will spur you, and so we walked and at night Amaro tells tall tales, after we tied the animal very well and gave him water and stayed there. Amaro says: "Once upon a time there was a cow named Tory and she farted and that's the end of the story," and we laugh a great deal and since there is nothing else to say we keep repeating, once upon a time there was a cow named Tory and she farted and that's the end of the story, which is all the same because Amaro forgets either the end or the beginning of the stories, sometimes he forgets the middle, sometimes the end, some- 95

times the beginning, and he says, this one I am going to start
from the middle, this one from the end, as the case may be.
Some of them he just remembers a little piece here, a little
piece there. At first one doesn't feel either like telling it or
listening to it, but after a while it makes no difference as long
as there is a story for us to give a middle and an end to or
then we don't give it anything and leave it alone. Amaro
remembers the story of an old woman who ate a little monkey and after two days she dropped him all in one piece in
a pisspot. How's that again, Amaro, ah-hum. How's that
monkey story again? And then it happened that the old
woman ate the monkey but the monkey came out in one
piece, I mean, she put it out whole, and how could this
monkey come out in one piece? Well, the story doesn't say,
it is because it is a very barefaced animal, if you eat it just
like that it comes out whole. Well then, he came out whole
and sang: I saw, I saw the old woman's ass, it is black and
white and yellow. How's that, Amaro, sing it again. I saw,
I saw, and I laugh very much, I laugh so much that I choke,
sometimes I laugh more than I ever thought I was able to. I
keep thinking about the old nag having a bellyache, and
what kind of an ass is it that's black and white and yellow?
How's that, Amaro, who taught the monkey this song, and
we sing all the time when we don't have anything to do
anyway and we laugh a lot and then we stop and start again
until we stop laughing and then all we do is squeeze ourselves a little, ay-ay. Ow, ow. Ahn. How's that, Amaro, and
he claps his hands and here comes the singing. Whoever
heard of that, a monkey coming out of that old woman's ass,
what do you know. I'll be damned. I'll be. It is black and
white and yellow, the poor old woman, it really must be like
that. It is never a good idea to eat monkeys, I tell you. Hey
Amaro, right now we could be in Tacaratu for the festival of
Our Lady of Health, can you imagine how we could be if we

were there now? Huh? Don't say it, what a good festival. There are some good people in Pernambuco, huh Amaro, at least people there are not cowardly, they are men, as in Alagoas. In Piauí, in Ceará, in Alagoas, sings Amaro, in Piauí, in Ceará, in Alagoas monkeys fly, monkeys fly, I like this one, what a hell of a monkey. How does this monkey fly, Amaro? Well, he has wings, monkey wings proper, wings of flesh like a bat's, those huge monkey wings, you have to see them. Stop lying, you keep talking untruthfully, no one ever told me about a flying monkey, a monkey is not an airplane. This is in Piauí, Amaro said, in Ceará and in Alagoas. All right, maybe over there, because it has never been said that a monkey from Sergipe could fly, I am sure about that. It is in Piauí, friend, says Amaro. All right, maybe over there. Now if one of those aviation monkeys came around here flapping his wings, we might even kill one of those beasts so we would have something to eat. Each house looks like a plateful of food but we had better keep away from the houses whose owners we don't know, there may be complications, the best thing to do is not to let our alertness down, I fear anything at a time like this. That is why if one of those Piauí monkeys decided to do a little flying around here it wouldn't be a bad idea. If we had a dog it would also be good because there is game in those bushes and in those hills there are opossum, but who can catch them? As a matter of fact, a slingshot would be better for hunting here than these guns, because if you shoot a scaled dove, a miserly scaled dove, nothing will remain of it, because these are all ox-killing guns. This teju lizard we hunted, we hunted without having intended to, because Amaro saw the burrow and rushed to it. I have never seen such patience before, he is like a hound, he lay there until the teju moved and he tried to catch it but the beast went back in, but Amaro riveted himself to the burrow, holding my Smith with the hammer pulled back, waiting. What patience, I don't know whether it comes of badness or of sainthood. I helped a little by digging a bit around the burrow to widen it and by then I don't know where the beast is, but after I left Amaro stood by very silently for hours and all I can say is that he ended up grabbing the beast and we ate it. I am going to keep its skin to give to a woman, Amaro said, women are very fond of teju leather. I myself have never seen any woman saying she was fond of teju leather. Amaro knows many things. Well, let him skin it. The meat looks like chicken only more stringy, and whole it looks like a big lizard and it doesn't taste much like anything, having been broiled on live coals without salt, and there was so much salt at the priest's place for the baptisms and I forgot to ask for some to bring along; when you are stupid you ask for your own death, there is nothing I can do. Unsalted teju. It is better than nothing and even the creature ate a few pieces. I thought he would be fussy but nothing of the sort, he ate up everything very well and would have eaten more if it had been given to him. Amaro, you are one hell of a teju hunter. I never hunted before, Amaro said, but I had a hole in my stomach, that's what I had. This teju tastes like the plague, we have to admit, but hunger is the best spice, and look here at this pox, how he seems to be so much at ease, see how he has changed, he even walks without any spurring. But this business of starving out here in the bushes, here in these wilds, this is not a good thing. Once in a while I catch the animal and inspect his gums. I peek to see how the situation is, I pinch his lips and take a close look, very good, yes senhor, we have fine gums here, no one could tell. Hey Amaro, if we get out of this fix I am going to be a dentist in Aracaju. No, not Aracaju nor Estância, because there they have other ones. But I can guarantee I am going to be the best dentist in Porto da Folha, or maybe in Muribeca, the people over there don't even know what a dentist is all about. We have fine gums here, ahn-well, it just may be I will pull out maybe four more to make a more complete job. The anesthetics are here, right here, look. Hum.

When it's green you can say it's good. It's all green. Sergipe is the greenest place there is when it's green, because sometimes it wilts and becomes brown and saddens. But when it's green like it is now it's the greenest there is and we see several colors in the woods, some greener, some less green, depending, and everything fragrant. Few bad woods, mostly good, restful woods, and one's eyes hover over them, it is a plentiful green. I say this to Luzinete, who is here lying down and we are in her home on the outskirts of Japaratuba, and she has a thing with me, she is taken with me and it's good to know that, because if I feel something she knows it, all I need to do is to raise my head. She is one devil of a big woman, two armlengths of a woman from top to bottom, seventy-five kilos of genuine woman well measured, a good woman and she wants me to leave her with child and to stay here to live and make more children. I said, if I make a child, what am I doing? I am staying here thinking about raising it. And then I tie myself down and stop and become full of roots, that is not for me. When I came in and started making myself comfortable it was early evening, and all I had time to do was to tell her what we were doing and to tie the animal well and to drop Amaro on a mat before she started tearing out my shirt and my pants and lodging me on top of her, and she sighed. Yes, I have not seen a woman for so much time I can't remember and besides, I said, I have not washed for some days, I have been out in the wilds, I must be smelling very foul indeed. And she said, it's the smell of the man I like the most, she said, and I started feeling that thing crawling up from inside my groin and it was like salvation, I mean, it was good and it even hurt, and she does it talking, she only 99 does it talking and making noises and saying: My baby, make me heavy, make me heavy, my little saint, make me heavy all over, fill up all of this woman, my mounting horse, oh my rod, and she coils around me until we mix. I like it. But I don't want to make you heavy, I already told you. Ahn-well, one day you will come to your senses and do it. I am only going to stay here for a couple more days, just time enough to rest, for I am going to get myself from here to Aracaju no matter what, there is nothing anyone can do, believe me. The eyes disturb me, it's true, because they are two shiny eyes, they are large and very slow that look at me deeply. Or they run all over me almost swelling me up, one can feel them. Not at that time, though, because at that time I feel like ripping her apart, to make her bulge out, and I watch it going in and out and the more it goes in the more I want it to go in and I want to open her up more and I raise my face and look at it going in again and go on stroking and pulling and biting, oh my God, I feel like hitting her a little and I ask her, do you want me to hit you, and she says, hit her because she is mine. Kill me, she says. Oh good Lord Jesus, vuct-vuct. Cafoot-cafoot. Hum.

There is almost no garrison in Japaratuba. Only when there is an election, then there is one. But if there is no election there is almost none, it's a small thing. Even when there is one, it's not much. They have a tall house with a slanted roof. It sits next to nothing on two sides. On one side there is a lawn which is always in the shade and the grass is cool and always a little damp because the women lay out their wash on it, bedsheets, pillowcases and everything. Out in front there is a doorstep that leads to a high door, more or less red and divided into two sections one of which is always open and there are some high windows of the same color. On the other side there is a house that belongs to someone I don't know, but between them there is a passage with a wooden gate and if you pass by there you get to the back yard, which is not much and has nothing on it, and you can leave it through an opening in a low wall with broken bottles on top of it. You can look at the ground next to the wall: There is always one who pisses next to the wall and if there is a red pepper tree nearby it is good for the peppers because they will get hotter. There are some tomato plants and some wide-leafed okra and some bell peppers and a few things like that and everything remains quiet for days and days, a little breeze stirring now and then and a person looking out the window without paying attention and spitting aside at times. But there was someone who crouched down there and planted okra, tomato and bell pepper and thinks about them, I am sure, because the plot is manured and clean, and every tomato has a father, one might say. The wall with the broken bottles can be jumped over, those pieces of glass won't cut anything, they get dull and colorless. Across the street there is a little square with more grass and weeds and around there no one can catch me, because from there you can head in every direction. Free on a horse, this very day, there is no one who can catch me, ah my name is Getúlio, my flower. And there are little mounds in this little square, wide but low, so that they don't hinder the hoofs of the horses and everything is fine. I don't know why I am going; it is just that I feel like raising a little hell, something like that, just to demonstrate. I don't really need one of those machines, and I don't really believe they have one in Japaratuba with the kind of threadbare garrison they have over there. Ahn-well, but I am going. I say that and I don't know why I say that; I think it is because I have not been feeling like leaving this place and my back arches up when I see I don't feel like leaving any longer. Not to mention Amaro, who keeps drinking goat milk like a newborn calf, he is going to thicken. He comes and goes and whistles and when he stops it's to look at the shotgun, it's a madness.

When I am lying down here looking at her bellybutton, I don't know anything. When I look at the bellybutton sometimes I feel like puffing on it, sometimes like sticking my tongue in it. When she is standing up it's better, because the belly makes a curve outward and one can see both things in better lines — the belly and the bellybutton. I keep thinking, here is this cow here, would you guess this cow is mine, I think it's excellent. When I look at your bellybutton, my girl, a hardness comes over me. That's why I don't feel like leaving and then I am going there to get that machine gun that someone told Amaro they have there, just to settle the argument and to see if they really have one, because I don't see many machine guns around here and that's the truth and besides I don't like them very much. I like guns that shoot with precision, that's what I like, and machine guns do a lot of destruction, I don't know. Well, I am going there. It is true that sometimes this bellybutton stays there like this and I don't feel like going. Sometimes I think, you know what I am going to do? I think this way: I stay right here and share her bed with her, she is a good woman, she is a woman like any other, only she is of the good kind. And I think this way: I tie up this trash over there and forget about him until his brain goes soft. Until he shrivels up. Or then I take care of him right away, I bury him and that's the end and I stay. I make one son, I make two sons, I make a heap of sons. She is a hell of a woman. If I say, I didn't like that stupid jug, she goes and breaks the jug and even says, I don't know how this devil of a jug ever got here, I can't endure this jug. And if when she is about to break it I say, what a pretty jug that is, has anyone ever seen a beauty of a jug as pretty as this, she picks up the jug, hugs it and says that a lovely jug such as this she has only because I like it. I could stay here all day making her pick up and put back the jug, but I feel sorry for her and I stop. It's better to look at the bellybutton, which is not one of those bellybuttons that bulge out that most people have and not one of the lumpy ones that come from crying too much as a child. Nor is it a bellybutton that turns inside too much and its borders get dark. It comes out a little on the upper side. Now, on the lower side lies a folded shell that when it goes up it turns outside and on this shell are the ends of the little hairs that come from below, almost impossible to see, and inside this shell it is always scented. It is a landscape. Sons, but the best thing about them is to make them. This was said to me by Dr. Renivaldo, who by the way owns a sugar mill around here, he told me he goes to Rio de Janeiro and sleeps with the best women, you should see the women. But do you know what I really like, Sr. Getúlio? I like it when it is sugar cane cutting time when the women are out in the field cutting sugar cane and I go riding a horse around the field and that is what I like, because there is one with a kerchief tied around her head cutting her sugar cane and bedewed with sweat and I come close, I don't even say anything. I pull her to the ground and she doesn't say anything either, she stays on the ground right there without paying attention and right then and there I deflower her and every time I like to think I am making her pregnant. Afterward I give her a house and a husband, if she wants one. But that is the way I like it, I greatly prefer it that way. Right, but this is something for sugar mill owners, I don't have a sugar mill and if I pull down a sugar-cane-cutting woman I will have to dispatch her whole family or else marry her or else let them dispatch me. I keep thinking I could take Luzinete to the sugar cane field and pull her down to the ground, but I feel a little silly. Leave things as they are, what's wrong with this bed? Now, sometimes I think it's a good idea to make a child, sometimes I think it is not. Because to make a woman pregnant is good, and to see her getting bigger every day, bigger, bigger, and to rub her with my hand, but then the child is born and then maybe it's not good anymore, because the damned child grows up and walks and asks questions many of which one does not wish to answer because it's discomfiting. And it's going to want so many things, I don't know. It becomes a person, maybe I won't be able to tolerate it. Besides, she is also here to ask questions herself, a woman after she bears a child becomes like a setting hen, she differs. I don't know. I'm not made for that, for staying here. What could I have, a few patches of land? And what could I do here? All I could do is to have a patch or two of land and work the land every day and go to town wearing tight shoes and see the woman farrowing and hear the child crying and grow cheerless. Then I die and that's that. I died. Oh shit, everything is like that, isn't this a lot of shit. For this reason I keep moving, because when I am moving I am not thinking and when I am acting I am not even knowing, that's it.

Which is the reason why I am swaddled in this black nightgown that belongs to Luzinete, I have it tucked inside my pants so no one will see that I am wearing skirts, and I am riding a black mule and took off my spurs so that they wouldn't jingle or shine under this half-moon up there and I am near the church listening to so many nighthawks it sounds like a nighthawk party. There are even responses, I think they are from father to son and from mother to daughter, from elder nighthawk to young nighthawk, hey what a bedlam we are going to have when I go in, yes we are. I am like a ghost with my face this way, believe me. Huh Amaro, if I had a gold front tooth now I would be the precise image of the very Devil, I myself wouldn't dare to look at myself in the mirror, especially with those goatsuckers hooting all over the place. There are owls in every large house around here but it is a good thing for they eat rats and other such pests, I even think owls are rather pretty if you look at them carefully, more than that rooster which can't be seen right now but which I know is perched on the roof, I don't know what for, because owls have those fluffy faces that I like, what I don't like are those goatsuckers that snap their bills and every snap makes the air tremble, have you ever seen that? He stands still and stares ahead and blinks his eyes in a way you hardly see and snaps his bill so loudly that it sounds like a hammer striking, holy Mary. I can't bear that kind, it seems to me they would take your finger off if you let them. And he probably can do it, because parrots can do it, did you know that? Well, they can. But there is nothing you can do about it, all you can expect at night are goatsuckers anyway. I hope they will eat all the bats that must be hanging around the hollows of the church. I hate bats. The only thing they are good for is to practice shooting at when they are all hanging upside down like bell clappers, but you can only shoot once, since after the first shot all the bats go crazy in the air and then no man can hit them. What a loathsome race, and they still go kwee-kwee-kwee when they are flying, a noise no Christian can bear. If I had it my way there would be no bats. That's why I don't like to visit caves and attics and if a bat touches me it's the same thing as giving me a glass of warm water, I throw up even my guts. Ahn-well, you lean against this place together with me and wait until the light in the tax collector's office goes out, because the collector stays up reading books. He must be studying about how to take even more money from people than he takes now, he and his little mustache, do you know him? You're not missing much, he's not worth the trouble of knowing him. I must look newsworthy all dressed up in black, the only thing I don't like is to be riding a mule. Have you noticed that this mule is farting, I only hope that there are no donkeys around here for him to want to mount now, 105 it wouldn't be funny. This mule, I know him, he is lewdness itself and here he is farting. Well, I'm glad this town will soon quiet down and become motionless and if it weren't for this muck of a collector with his burning lantern I could already have gone in that house to pick up the goods. You don't think that going in this one house to pick up this one machine gun is stealing, because I am not a thief. It may be a crime but it is not stealing, because taking something from a garrison may be a crime but it's not stealing. It may be whatever they please, nothing sticks to me, I am I and the devil can be the rest, screw it. Now this collector stays there dragging his slippers on the floor and reading his nonsense and interfering with other people. The reason I am waiting is because after he puts it out it is difficult to light up again and if he is still up perhaps I will have to shoot him with this cannon of a shotgun and then all we would have would be a collector's little bits, man I am just crazy to see that thing shooting, it must be an uproar. But look, don't pull back those two hammers now because this damn thing can't be adjusted and these mules might get startled and then you will shoot even the sky, which will not turn out well, it may even blow a hole through a saint's hat or some such thing. I keep thinking in my black dress, what if I went away to be a bandit if they still had bandits. There was a time when I hated bandits, I think I did until yesterday, the day before the day before yesterday, before before, but now I don't any longer, what can I do. Well then, I could be a bandit, then. If there were bandits. Inasmuch as there are not, I stay here. Hey Amaro, whee, hey blossom, if I were Lampião, would you be Maria Bonita, his wife? How about that, hum. I said it once, I say twice and thrice, you are yellow in excess, you stay there chewing up that leather strap with the appearance of a goat, it's hard to believe. I am getting tired of waiting here, I am going to blast through that door mule and all any minute now and wreck the garrison and haul the things out. I am better than the king of Hungary, all in black here. I wish I were riding a horse, not one of those lame-legged nags like the ones you see around here, but one of those horses whose hoofs seem to be made of cork, a horse that bites the bit, lowers his face and blows smoke through his nostrils, it might be one of those, and me better and handsomer and braver than the king of Hungary, waiting for combat. No one can stop me, I will do it on the mule anyway, I want to see it. I am thinking: If one of these bastards in the garrison knows me, he is going to die, so that he won't go around the world testifying. But after I do it I will say, why, brother, don't worry, you can say it was Getúlio, say I was the one who broke open this whole damned place, rapped the heads of the whole band of harlots here, pissed in the living room and lunged out at the bushes like thundersparks, what a man. Ahn. I will fix anybody who cries out or tries to show bravery. I think I am becoming more evil, that's good. The place is full of queers in there and that's the way it's going to be, I don't even want to know what people are going to say afterward. I couldn't care less.

When I came bursting out the door, carrying a string of rifles slung over my shoulder by their straps, Amaro darted out from behind the trees dragging one mule and riding the other and making a hell of a noise and the mules galloping in that mulish way with their rumps going up and down and the collector's window went all lit up and there were women yelling from every corner and a man came out in his underwear from inside and pointed a Winchester our way and I shouted, "Look out for your life Amaro!" and Amaro didn't converse, he twisted the mule's bridle rope around his ankle and somehow managed to swirl around the straw saddle and raised the shotgun right at the sniper and it was only once: Toon! and it didn't hit him, it hit the roof above him and there were pieces of clay flying everywhere and smoke and Amaro almost slides down his saddle, that thing recoils with a strength almost equal to the shot itself, you have to be a big priest like that one to be able to shoot it without falling over backward. All of this happened very fast because I was moving at top speed, since there were many more soldiers in there than I had expected and they almost grabbed me and the only reason they didn't grab me was that maybe they thought I was a ghost and because they all sleep without precautions. When I went in, that disgrace of a door, which stays ajar because of the heat, creaked loudly and then I stopped and peeked inside. I would have given anything to have a gold tooth because there was a smooth-haired black sleeping in there who woke up when the door creaked and if I had had a gold tooth I wouldn't have had to touch him, all I would have had to do was to flash an illuminated smile at him and he would have crumbled down with fear, blacks of this type are terribly fearful of the Devil because they are closer to him, I guess. I said: Sleeping in your bed of twigs, you bastard, now see this fish knife I brought along with me that I left poisoning inside a dead rat for two weeks and which has a fishhook near the tip for me to extract a piece of your gut when I pull it out of your belly in order to have this piece of gut with liquor, because if there is one good thing, it is to eat the tripe of a troublemaking bastard fried in wheat flour as an appetizer. I said it in his ear so as not to make noise, and in fact I had a fish knife with me, one of the best, which I borrowed from Luzinete and spent the whole day sharpening, but it didn't have a hook for I am not like people from Pernambuco who enjoy eating the guts of their enemies, and I didn't even feel like bleeding that black who was turning whiter and whiter with so much fear and I even had to put my hand on his mouth so he wouldn't yell his head off and he was panting and trembling in his legs, but

I pressed the tip of the fish knife and twisted it, twisted it, I pressed the tip of the knife against his shirtless ribs and kept twisting, however without really stabbing, only the very tip until it became red and he felt it. Look, you pox, if you so much as peep I will barbecue you this moment, where do you keep the guns here? And then I had to wait for a while because when I let go of his mouth he seemed to want only to pray and I kept watching him, I almost sat in a chair they have there to watch him fidget. Who are you, senhor? Who, me? I am the ghost of your slave grandfather's owner, son of a mare, and your time has come! But he kept positioning himself to pray, he was trembling like mush and then I helped him stand up, he was so small and weak I can't describe him, and I said, just take me to the locker because I want to pick up a few things, you must be from Bahia, black and shaking like that you can only be from Bahia. Then he said, for the love of God I am from Muribeca, and I almost laughed out loud because there is another Muribecan, called Amaro, waiting out there and he must not be doing much better than this one here, out there among the owls in the dark, holding a mule and a shotgun. All right, you are from Muribeca, now show me where the things are, and I kept pushing him with his arm twisted sideways like this and we got to a locker and who said there was anything like a machine gun, there were only some old rifles that I began picking up and hanging from my arm whereupon what seems to be a rain of heads comes in, about four in all, one behind the other, one wearing a hat, and one said, what the hell is going on in there? It's the Devil, I said, and I thought it wise to back up because they were many and there could be more guns than those I had picked up, and I had to back up and then I raised my foot and kicked the black's butt with the tip of my boot and pushed him on top of the others and dashed out and that was when I appeared at the door thinking, why the hell do I want to come here at this time of night to grab a couple of old guns and risk getting shot needlessly? I don't do only what I have to, but I also do what I want to, that's it, and I saw Amaro carrying on by the door, only he in his haste had unloaded the two barrels on the man's roof and maybe somebody else has a gun and wishes to open fire, so that I just threw myself in Amaro's direction and jumped on the mule which was in great agitation as it was and Amaro was still holding the bridle's rope wrapped more or less around his shin I don't know how, and an awesome smoke and a lot more men were coming out of the garrison house barging into each other and the women screaming ceaselessly.

Then I said, "Get the hell out of here, Amaro, now it's all or nothing, I don't even want to look." He didn't say a thing, he just unwrapped the rope from around his foot, and I only had time to mount the mule, hit him with my heel and ride out like a bullet down the square's path. I am lucky that this mule already knows the way, you just let him go and he goes well, because I have yet to see a mule that enjoys hearing shooting or crossing a bridge because none of them cross of their own free will, I think they are afraid to fall off, and here I go, better than the king of Hungary, I don't even want to look back. We have a good stretch ahead of us and the best thing to do is to go through the woods, anyway the black must be saying it was an apparition and there will be plenty of time before anyone follows us, especially since the moon is wilted and lightless and it's dark. Good, Amaro, go on keeping your head low because of any tree branches there may be ahead and do your little swimming and you can even close your eyes for the mounts never miss and will get home in no time. Amaro asked if I had seized something and I said I wanted to seize the son of a bitch who had said there was a machine gun in the garrison house of Japaratuba, all there was were these old rifles and a few bandoliers I didn't even bother to look at, these trinkets may not even fire anymore. Ahn-well, I did it because I wanted to do it and I liked the way that baby almost knocked all of the man's house down, come to think of it, what else could he expect with that repeater pointed at us. When I left I even tripped on my way out and kicked a piece of iron that was sticking up from the ground with my big toe, and when I left and shouted, "Come on, Amaro, because I killed twenty-three in there," I could swear you believed me, but even if they were not twenty there were a lot of those lizards in there, because all you could see were heads popping up. And people still say I'm no good. If I were bad I would have stopped right then and there and would have picked off the whole gang of queers at the tip of my rifle, which would have been easy, they were all scampering just like lizards, just like game on a barren plain, that's how it was. But I didn't aim at any of them. Now, I can't deny I would like to halt here and wait, I really can't, because it would be very easy, but in the first place I have a runniness in my nose which may be catarrh which this mist makes worse, and second, no one will chase us after all, those yokels don't look like a good garrison, and third, this night-gown of Luzinete's keeps blocking my parts and these frills seem to scratch you, I don't know how women can put up with wearing these garments with all the splinters they have. You can say that I once dressed like a woman when I entered the garrison house in Japaratuba, when I entered the garrison of Japaratuba, and there right in front of all the men they say they have there, and should there be more, in front of every man they have there, I went in, I opened things up and I picked up everything I cared to and that's it, brothers and sisters. I did not have to do any of those things, it was just for the hell of it, the Lord be praised.

I tell you, Luzinete, looking out the window like this, I

could stay here. But there are times when you can stay, there are times when you can't accept that. That's the way it is. Just like there are times when you are pleased by the playing of an accordion, and there are times when you feel like beating up the accordionist. It's the same thing. That's why at certain times, when I have my elbow on the windowsill and you come back from washing clothes with your fingers still crinkled from the water and stained with bleach and I gaze at the greenery, at those times maybe. For what happens afterward? The following happens: I start finding something of interest in everything, and I become very lazy. And I know there will be nothing to do, neither today nor tomorrow. And I know that on your return we can expect to eat because things to eat are sure to come our way and we can say what time we want the food to appear. And a person can sit chatting as much as he pleases, having a few things to drink, and all of a sudden there appears a novelty: A crab. Or two. A person becomes very pleased with that crab; you boil it and we suck its legs and sit there and it's such a long afternoon and then we eat as much as we please and go to sleep. Tell me if it is not so. It certainly is. What a cool breeze, huh? Can anyone disturb us, huh? A lot of eating and a lot of sleeping, and everybody else can go to hell, good-by. But when we are not doing that we have to talk and then there is nothing to do and a person has to walk up and down minding one thing here and one thing there, shaking a leather strap in the air and kicking stones. Which is impossible, I don't want it that way. Tell me, shall we take up banditry? I know there is no banditry anymore, but if there were would you come with me? No, you wouldn't, you're the kind of woman who likes better a child in the belly and a man in the bed and a natural death. Not I, because there is a line in my hand that cuts across the biggest line, which says violent death. That's a fact, you can't run away from it. It's better that way, it hurts less and gives less trouble. I believe in that death, because I can't think that I am going to become old and toothless and my hand is going to quaver. One thing that doesn't exist is an old Getúlio, there is only the whole man Getúlio. I can't exist with a flabby mouth, saying in my time this and in my time that. It is true that there are certain old men who are still men, but they are from the old times, not these times. In the old times there was magic, I think. If there were still banditry, I would go and be a bandit with a hat of silver stars and I would be called Bogey Dragon and would speak little and do much. When I entered places, I would enter stomping my feet. When I rode, I would ride with my chest swollen and my face up, always looking ahead. When I marched, I would march swinging my body and smelling the wind. When I ate, I would eat in big hunks taking the knife to my mouth. I would be the biggest bandit in Brazil, the greatest captain of bad men in Brazil and I would have the most troops. And they wouldn't call me sergeant, they would call me captain. Or they would call me major. If I cut off a lieutenant's head, I would pull out his teeth and make myself a necklace. All lieutenants whose heads I cut off I would pull out their teeth. And every place I went I would roar very loud to break windowpanes and drink two casks of liquor at a time and eat two goats alone or else a calf and would blow trees out of the ground and when I pounded with my rifle butt on the ground the ground would tremble all over and the fruit would fall down. Bogey Dragon, you can call me.

Luzinete, what I am really going to be is a state representative and smoke cigars. Amaro may drive my car, I will let him. To be a state representative you don't need anything. If I were a representative, you would come along, wouldn't you? To dress up all lordly, and you would learn how to talk stiffly, wouldn't you? Then when I got to the House with this piece of junk tied by the neck I would tell my fellow party members, look at this gift here, you know what I am going to do with this gift? I am going to hang this gift for everybody to see, and I would hang him from the leg of the table. And I would say: This stretch of tongue hanging out I give to the governor's wife, who talks too much and doesn't notice it. This broken neck I will give to the doctors of medicine, so they can have the chance to see a well-broken neck. These hanging arms I give to the people, so the people can hug me. These wobbling legs I also give to the people, so the people can walk. And I would carry on like that, I would give away the whole piece of trash and then I would go out to the radio station and I would put a handkerchief in my pocket and wear a linen suit and brown and white round-tipped shoes and I would play cards for money. Don't you think I would do well as a representative? I think I would, believe me, I would be a good representative. That is, if I wanted to be a representative. You remember the chief? He is also a representative now, I think. He told me to go get this trash in Paulo Afonso and now they came to tell me not to take him to Aracaju anymore, by order of the chief. I don't believe that, do you? It may be, but now I am going to take him no matter what. Yesterday I said I was going to, today I don't know for sure, because this place here makes me soft, but how can I live like this? It's like I say, many times at a time like this a person thinks the world stops. But it doesn't stop, a person knows better. There are a lot of people moving, and I am here in the middle, motionless. But motionless like a fish near river rocks, if you move close to him he will snap his tail and vanish. Because that's the way I am. See what lazy people, see what stupid people. I go there, I pick up this pure garbage, I tickle the ribs of a smooth-haired black soldier with a knife and stay nearby as if nothing had happened and nothing happens. Then I could die of old age, couldn't I? I could. I could stay here and every year make you pregnant just right for the boy to come in January, which is the beginning of the year and therefore more appropriate. Women would not be born, only a lot of males and I would give them real male names and after that we would take these lands around here and we would organize some troops with more men and we would be masters of the world here, each son finding himself a woman and each woman bearing more men and we giving the orders, and when I died, grandfather of everybody, direct or indirect father, they would bury me here and put on top the Lord on the Cross and those who passed by would say, that cross belongs to the deceased and if you don't cross yourself he will come and get you. Think of all those men, they would be Stud Santos Bezerra, Wickedness Santos Bezerra, Abusive Santos Bezerra, Knocks-All-Down Santos Bezerra, Eats-People Santos Bezerra, Backscrewer Santos Bezerra, Bursts-Pussies Santos Bezerra, Blooddrawer Santos Bezerra, Overcomes-Horses Santos Bezerra, everybody. You would appreciate that, I think. One fine day Overcomes-Horses Santos Bezerra was riding down the road when he met a mule train crossing a path that only allowed the passage of one at a time, and Overcomes-Horses said to the men of the mule train: "I request passage, for I am more of a man than you and your mule train can very well wait for me to pass, in a slow pace, very calmly and whistling, all the more because I am king of the Crown of Sergipe." And the mule driver said: "You, senhor, may think that you are more of a man than ourselves and think that you are king of the Crown of Sergipe, but we actually don't think so, as a matter of fact we think we are more of men than you are and for this very reason you, senhor, will remain there sitting quietly, waiting until the last of the mules pass, so that you will then be able to pass, and this if I see fit." It was then that Overcomes-Horses said: "See here, you sallow earthworm, listen well, squashy worm, mind what I am telling you, turdy bug, pay attention, easily-roped ox, head-lowerer, heed because I speak only once, sparrow heart: When I was born some archangels came down to bear me gifts and Saint Roman to crown me and I was so strong that my bed was made of steel and silver and when I wept it rained here and in Bahia and I was fed the milk of four golden Dutch cows and I can tell you: Do you see this arm here? Well, with this arm I will push this hill of six hundred thousand times fifteen kilos down on top of your head. And if I bite you I will chop your head off with a single snap. If I spit and it hits your eye I will blind you. If I clap my hands I will leave the whole train deaf. And if I kick this lead mule she is going to end up where the devil lost his boots, that is what I am telling you." And then he remained on his spirited horse, upright, cocky and waiting for an answer. There were only shades near him, because the sun was no fool to come close to him. Well, then the mule driver pulled out a pistol and fired against Overcomes-Horses Santos Bezerra and the other mule drivers fired too and it was the most ill-considered thing they did in their whole lives, because it was thus that Overscomes-Horses caught the bullets in his teeth and spat them out and said: "With these bullets, pustulent one, you busted out a sliver of my upper-right-hand wisdom tooth, and if there is one tooth I hold dear it is this upper-right-hand wisdom tooth and that is exactly the reason why I shall apply punishment to you," and then he picked up a mule in each hand by the tail and spun them and spun and spun and attacked the train with the mules and each one who got up was muled. Then he grabbed the whole train and threw it all where the devil lost his boots. You see the kind of son I have? Invincible.

VII

Then I am here sitting down on this prairie with these ashes I put on my head and all the paths I dug with my feet, walking in circles for I don't know how long and pounding on my chest and gurgling with my throat and I roared so loud it was heard in the whole state of Sergipe in every direction and up and down to the hollow of the world which boomed, I let out the greatest roar ever heard on earth, because it was now that I felt it. First I sat on a tree stump and slipped my head between my outstretched legs and remained sitting for twenty-two hours, fifty-eight hours, I remained sitting for more hours than anybody ever sat, and I didn't move at all. I stared at the ground but without seeing anything, just the single-colored ground. After that I stood up and I felt an anger, the greatest anger ever felt in the whole state of Sergipe, I felt an anger thick as blood and heavy as five hundred sacks of sugar and hot like an ember the size of a cattle herd. And being up I stretched out my arm with my fist closed, I stretched out the other arm and I pounded on my chest so much that it thundered and the leaves from the trees came falling down and then I walked, with each step as long as two armlengths, and when I walked at each step clouds of dust went up which turned into mud with the tears that came out of me. Then I looked around and saw nothing. I strained my eyes and saw nothing and I wished I had a very big sword so that with this sword I could bring down all things that stood in front of me or behind me, riding a black horse whose sweat would stink so much that it would kill and on this horse I would go down Cotinguiba River with my sword and would stick my sword into the river and kill the fish and split up the water and fill up the world with water and eat everything and make everything disappear. And I. I strained my eyes this way and could see nothing really, I was just feeling and I put out the night fire with my hands and picked up the ashes that remained and rubbed them on my head and face and didn't want to do anything else for a long time, because I became sorrowful, and then I let out a roar that was heard in the whole state of Sergipe, the ground shook and I sat down again.

When I saw him he was motionless with his eyes open, in the same position he took to hit the barrels of the gun, lower them and load them. I mean, with his right hand still up because it could never come down, for his sleeve had caught on a nail on the wall and stayed there. What I first saw were his eyes because I was looking out the window to cover the entrance, luckily no one could come from the back as it is a high cliff, and I was even beginning to think it was a light job, since as they appeared on the road we could hit them easily, they would be easy targets, even if they were shooting our way and taking big hunks out of the wall, outside and inside. In the beginning we thought we might stick the creature's head out of the window, but they were shooting so much and making such a din that it seemed the world was going to fall down, so if I put his face at the window they would surely make holes all over his face at once and he would die and lose his usefulness. Sons of bitches, they must have asked for help from the whole town to catch me like a stray calf, only they are not going to catch me, they may catch their mothers but not me. Well, I was keeping my eyes on the window resting the gun to blast the chest of one who was coming sideways and I wanted my shot to strike his ribs and then Amaro's gun stopped banging. I say, what are you doing, Amaro, if you are out of ammunition take one of those garrison guns because there are plenty and he made no answer. Nothing, so when I managed to place two slugs in the wretch there who started letting go of the fence post, letting go, letting go, until I saw that it was the last time he would let go of anything in his life, I looked sideways and saw Amaro's eyes.

Before that he was fine, in fact he was excellent, because he had learned how to handle the gun well, which is not easy. It looks easy but it is not easy, it calls for practice. But it was he, who was sitting on the floor with both knees up and rubbing the gun's barrels and chewing on a blade of grass like his mind was somewhere else, it was he who first saw something arriving and then he stood up without saying anything and went out to look at the pathway. Just a minute, he said, and leaned against the side of the door, spat out the grass and remained there. This door is going to open in a little while, he said, and I am going to make a celebration. Ahn-well, I said, we have a disturbance, and I stood up, seized an instrument and looked almost sideways through the window and in fact over by the bend a bunch of pestilential characters were waiting for something. This one Amaro is going to get must have boasted of bravery up there and now is coming here. Hey, you bunch of cheap spinsters, prepare yourselves to die! Hum-hum. I thought, but I didn't say it, that it was lucky that they had stopped up there because we were not ready in here. I myself didn't hear a thing, I was thinking about brown sugar and Luzinete was picking some lice. Everything was very quiet, we didn't even know what time it was, there was no after and no before, it was a stillness and I was too lazy to think about when I should leave to take the creature to Aracaju, I don't know, I don't know. Amaro keep track of this one who is squeezing himself by to see I don't know what in here, maybe he is not sure we are in here and comes on a mission of espionage. I held the gun in my hand leaning the barrel against the wood of the window, hey spitfire, hey spitfire. Let's go. Amaro didn't show anything, only his hammers were pulled back and the left hand had its fingers half white from grabbing the two barrels. And when the man started pushing the door and Amaro was behind to push the barrels on his back so we could make some inquiries of him, that bastard of a trash, who was tied but wasn't gagged, cried with that gummy voice: "Watch out, there's a man behind the door." Well, he didn't cry out twice, the vile one, because I went over to him and gave him a couple of belts on his face with the barrel of my gun and after that I pushed his face down on the floor with the sole of my boot and kept rubbing it in, rubbing it in, until he went limp and I gave him maybe two boot-tip kicks on his kidneys to complete it and I think he thought it better to quiet down, it was either quieting down or a lot of explaining. And I said to Luzinete, if he moves even his big toe break this jug on his head and if he makes too much trouble pour kerosene on him and set fire to him, this way he will learn. She then crouched down and kept watch over him, holding a batch of those matches that you can strike on the sole of your shoe, with the lamp close by and also the jug. The first time I use the jug. The second time I set fire. And she thought maybe the best thing to do would be to pour the kerosene right away so as to be sure to have time when the time comes, so she poured half of what was in the lamp on his pants and stayed there squatting, looking like nothing. That one is a special woman.

But the man who was coming in, it seems he had no time to change his intent on account of the cry, or else he didn't even hear it because the junk cried out weakly, and he went on pushing the door. And that was when Amaro gave a little jump aside, stood in front of the man and hit both triggers at once quite in the right direction and all you could see was the man's face disappearing and there were slivers of head all over. Man, if you had hit the notary in this fashion there would be no one to notarize in Japaratuba for more than twenty years, hail Mary, the man made almost a full flip when he received the blow. The man jumped up, I mean, he didn't jump up, it was because of the impact of the gun, and he ended up in prickland. With nothing almost from the chest up, he was like a painting. Then I thought, if they really had a machine gun in that goddamned garrison I would not need anything else, I could take care of the rest from here, but that couldn't be, so when I opened fire the band started spreading out and it seemed there were more men coming all the time. You would think I was Lampião, with so many people out to get me, how about that? Well, now the thing to do is to hold on until we find a way to get out and it seems there are not too many ways because these people are not the kind that give up and they will hang on until they come in here, but I am I and I want to see that party of swollen bellies come in here. They are going to back out, they have to back out, come, come. And I used to say you had a soft heart, huh Amaro? No one would recognize you know, my bird. That one must be called Secundino of the Thick Headfat because of that lump on top of his head, as if it had waves. That's pure lard. Now, this Secundino came shooting very well, zigging and zagging and thinking himself a great combatant. He must have had a couple before coming over here and I can

121

see him talking: I will come back here bringing this bastard dragged by a horse, with no breeches, no vest, no jacket and no stripes and his grave is going to be the dust he is going to eat before dying. It is going to be an internal grave. This he must have said. But take heed, Secundino of the Thick Headfat, I am the one who is going to bury you and I can even afford to let you come from up there like a monkey with these leaps of a circus clown and leaps never decided a man's fate, I never tolerated these leapers, I can assure you. Secundino look at the sky, remember that cow of a mother you have, because I am going to make a hole in you, such a hell of a hole that you, senhor, will leave us through it, praise Our Lord Jesus Christ, I am the Bogey Dragon, Eater of Hearts. I am standing here at the window corner just watching him hopping around. Let him hop: Better start picking the bumelia of Heaven, the cactus of Hell, hum-hum. And then the mouth fills up with water a bit, like when you prick a boil and pull out the skin off its middle, as he leaped to the left-hand side and I chose to get him midway in his leap. Good-by Secundino of the Thick Headfat Soares de Azevedo da Paixão, you can say you died in the air. You died neatly; when you came down you moved no more. That other one, look Amaro, you should hit him in the belly with a first-class shot because that is a watery belly, made of pig fat, of hot lamb fat, that is not worth anything. A man like that is pregnant and his name is Feeble Fluffy Fabriço of the Flour and when you hit his belly it is going to be like the River Vaza-Barril swollen up and making water flow on all sides, the problem is that he lies down all the time and offers only a piece of his shoulder. Offer more, Fafá, hey. Show that little belly, my dear. Here! Luzinete, afterward we must send the bills for repairing the wall plaster to the garrison house, because they are practically taking out all of the plaster, you see that? See what big chunks of plaster, look here, what do you know, they are pretty confident. Amaro, if that pox raises his belly you let him have it in the belly, because at this distance the lead spreads well and the wind is not enough to weaken it. Even if that thing lives, there is no doctor who can pick hundreds of pellets from a paunch and it hurts like a beauty, all the more in those folds, his belly must be full of folds. Fluffy, hey Fluffy. Here! Look there Amaro, he is starting to stand up. Look there Amaro, he is sweating all over, he looks like a pregnant ass, look at his face, have you ever seen anybody that fat? Look there Amaro, what a greasy face, every one of those sweat beads looks like a jack fruit seed. When he passes by the mangaba tree you watch him, there is no need to hurry, because being fat like that he is going to place his hand on the tree, take off his hat and wipe his brow. All that water must already be getting into his eyes and smarting. The best thing would be to hit this ox's backside, except that he won't turn it to us, that's natural. But see: Didn't I tell you he was going to lean against the mangaba tree? Now there, look at the cannon, it looks like an army piece, let him have it, Amaro! Hum. He is going to remain there wriggling for a while, let him. There are some black ants on that mangaba tree, the kind that stink, and they are going to bother him even more, forget about him. I said he was going to lean against the tree. I spoke and I said it and it happened. If we leave here we go to the ground vines, because the ground vines will fight for us, isn't that right? Here come two other ones, a skinny one and a stocky, swarthy one. Don't you think this is easiness itself, Amaro? If they stormed us, then I don't know, because we would have to shoot very fast, but one by one like this, or two by two, the more they come the more of them won't go back. This swarthy one, his name is Dried Banana Chico, because his face seems to be all wrinkled. I think they rubbed a genipap on his face for it to become all black like that, that 123 is an ugly son of a bitch, huh Amaro. Leave this one to me because he is coming right down my line of fire, he looks like a water chicken waddling by a pond. The thin one is named Paulino Pious Pain, because of two things. First he looks like a regular novenagoer, wouldn't you say so? He does. He makes the women sing to purge his sins, because he is afraid to die and go to Hell. Second he walks in a twisted way, see if he doesn't look like he had a rheumatic pain when he was little. So, very well, you ram two cartridges in there once again and get Paulino wherever you can get him, he must have a full twenty novenas on him. Tell me something, the barrels of this contraption, don't they overheat? Get the twisted little man and I will get Dried Banana, and prepare yourself because there must be one hell of a crowd down there. Look there Amaro, shame on you, the twisted one untwisted all of himself, I think you didn't get a full hit, because he has already taken off and disappeared. His real name must Stumbling Stray, because there he goes like a stray heifer, but the dark one, I think that when he went down he went down for good. So that you can expect the fusillade to increase, oh plague, there is a heap of men over there that will never end, you have to see it to believe it. And this smoke hangs on because the weather is wet. If it were dry it would be better, there wouldn't be so much smoke. Maybe this whole area is full of men, behind these. In short, either we go or we stay. I am going and show me who can stop me.

Then when I saw Amaro's eyes still and him looking at nowhere with his arm hanging from the nail, I saw that he had been killed and in the beginning I didn't feel anything. I only looked again and said, "Luzinete it seems they got Amaro. Wouldn't it be a good idea to hang this animal by his feet, it was because of him that they killed Amaro, wasn't it?" But I had no time to do anything else because the fusillade was going on and I had to hold on and I remained like that until it was about two o'clock and it seems that they sent out for reinforcements, because as far as I know they must have left about four watching the pathway, maybe more, so as not to allow anybody to go out. "In about half an hour those reinforcements will be here, won't they?" "About that," said Luzinete, and she wasn't afraid. I looked again at Amaro dead. Luzinete said, "When you were shooting out the window I wanted to close his eyes, but they didn't close, they will have to stay this way." "Yes," I said, "they will have to stay that way. Yes, they will have to." Then she said, "He was like a brother to you," and I said, "I think he was, he really was, I think he was, and I think that in this world there were only him and you for me, this I believe. I am brokenhearted," I said, "life is shit." I sucked air in: If you are alive you are dead, that's the truth. "Say a chaplet, Luzinete. Say a rosary. Just the other day he was saying prayers at the priest's, he knows all the prayers." "No, he doesn't know, he knew," Luzinete said, "and why don't you finish all those accursed people once and for all and go on with your mission?" "Right," I say, "if only I were an airplane. If only I were an elephant. There are a lot of men out there, and if I went there, before I could say ouch they would take care of me right and proper and then who would take this poxy person to Aracaju, you can't do it for sure." "Well, if you stay here you also won't be able to go out." "This I know," I said, "but also I don't know. Something always happens. Look, I am a different man, not different the way you think, but I am different because I feel different, it is another thing. I can tell you something that I thought when I was over there at the priest's, but listen to it silently because if you laugh I will beat you up: I am Getúlio Santos Bezerra and my father   125 was tough and my grandfather was tough and in these back-lands here there is no one as tough as I am. And if a ram comes up I will sock his forehead and he will die. And there are more things, but I won't say them now. These things are not to be talked about, maybe. Hum, it is no use. I am I. My name is a verse: Getúlio Santos Bezerra, and now and then I think that as long as there is no one better than I everything that happens to me is better than what happens to anybody else. Hum. I don't know, I think I think too much, it's no use." "Your name is a verse," Luzinete said, "and you are never going to die." "This is a fact. I will take this man back right now. There is this crowd outside, isn't there? If I were the kind to be led around by the nose I would have gotten rid of all this trouble already. There is no one after me by now. But since I am greater than anything, because I am like that and was raised like that, anything can happen and just the same I am going to take this piece of junk to Aracaju if I have to drag him. I said I would take him and I will and nothing can stop me, I am telling you. After that anything can happen, it's not necessary to grub all over Sergipe to find me because I am free and a man and I want to see things, because the worst that can happen to me is to die and that is not the worst thing. The worst thing would be to be a day laborer in any sugar mill. The worst thing is to be nobody, but I saw it when I was at the priest's, when I talked to the men and Amaro was pointing that instrument inside the church, I saw what I am, and I am I, and that's why I am going to take this animal back and no one is going to stop me and if they do I will destroy everything." "I know," Luzinete said looking at me. "But why don't you finish these buzzards once and for all?" "I told you, something has to happen, I am not an airplane. It may be at night, it may be I will slip out at night and disappear; there is no moon out tonight and I am not a firefly to glitter in the dark." "There are some bombs here," Luzinete said, "there are some bombs here which belong to the man who was living together with my sister and who used to work at a stone quarry." "What bombs?" "A couple of bombs," she said, "and each one looks like a roll and they come in fives or half a dozen, you just light them and throw them. And if you separate them you can throw about five times or half a dozen, which opens a passage and leaves nothing. They are fine bombs."

Do you see that, shining in the dark, pox? That thing shining blue, that is a plant by the name of cunanã, which is like vines. That is your hell, it has always been. But as for myself they are my stars and I know my way around there because I was born here and this is my land. Now it's all mine, because everybody died who was any good. All your fault, and you have nothing to do with this land, I can assure you. Well, are you seeing those glimmers? They are my glimmers of the wilds and if I wanted to I could shine too and I could marry Princess Firefly and would fly. But I won't do that, I will take you to Aracaju and what will happen there I don't know. Luzinete went up with the bombs, nothing could be found of her amid the rubble and the dirt. Is that satisfactory? Well then. And so. I couldn't stay there, that I couldn't do. There were moments when I thought I could, but that was because I forgot who I was. When I remembered, I remembered the roads and these prairies you can find around here, this and that spot, a sugar cane field and a drought forest, this was what I remembered, this melon cactus. This is all one greenness but nobody can feel it, only those who can feel. Now, as my wife she could stay there all the time because I would go there once a year and with one single stroke of my rod I would make her pregnant for all of her life, enough for her to bear and bear to the end, every baby so big their navel cords would have meters of cord and the pregnancy would last twelve months, because I am built 127

like a jackass here, I am built like the biggest of animals, and
if I come on this ground fruit trees will sprout. The ground
is like my mother, pox. You pox, male whore, pox, pox, pox,
you big queer. Names lose their strength when I call you
names and that is why I am going to invent a heap of names
to call you and from now on everyone will use these names.
Aboormish pustulent, violated in Hell, disfrickumbered
friffolill of the boiling oil. And I will invent more. If she had
survived I'm not saying I would have stayed, but it would
have been all right with me. But I would go there and would
make her pregnant with just one stab and she wouldn't even
need to eat because she would be like earth, needing only
rain. That would be all she would require. And how about
my sons, pox? Carniculated of the burragilla, retroquelent of
the muckolamud. Don't you dare answer, because I will take
your life in the worst way, taking two years and a half, each
day cutting off a few grams of your flesh, think about it,
don't be presumptuous. She used to be my woman, now she
is the moon. Do you know, senhor, that my woman is now
the moon? She became the moon when she exploded with
the bombs and the men who were there are Beelzebubs and
will live under the ground for as long as I want them to and
I will always want it. Now, Amaro. I don't care what anybody says when they see me with these ashes on my face,
and whoever says something I don't like I will eat his soul,
when I look at things I make them shrivel, I can turn a person
into a sausage. When I roared so loud it was heard in the
whole state of Sergipe from the São Francisco River to the
state of Bahia from corner to corner, it was because of
Amaro, who was my brother. Luzinete is the moon, but how
about Amaro? He is nothing. He is nothing because he died
and stayed there with his eyes open. He was small, but he
was a man, more of a man than nine hundred thousand of
your kind and with this same gun which belonged to the

priest and after that to him and after that to me and I keep it on my back and no hand but mine can touch it or the person will die, with the very same gun I can face whatever appears, I can do it. If a batallion comes I will stand up to them. If a giant comes I will strangle him. Now I have a pain in my chest and sometimes I can't even catch my breath and until now I have been weeping mud and I spent some hours without desiring anything, without being able to raise my hand, without seeing anything.

He used to be a driver, listen, and now he is nothing. How is it possible to think of this? And keep quiet and march well because every time I say Amaro I also mean to say praise Our Lord Jesus Christ and you think without saying it, but you have to think for real because I am looking at your face, you must think, may such a good Lord be forever praised, and you have to think like this: Such a good Lord Amaro may he forever be praised, such a good Lord Amaro, such a good Lord Amaro, march or I will make holes in your back with the spur, and thank me for not riding on you and thank me for not burying you in the ground head down with a hollow stalk in your nose to let the air in, thank me, you bastard! Ay, ay, ay, ay. You can say I am dirty but this is ashes and ashes are so burned that they are clean and I will not wipe these ashes off my face. I didn't even see when he got shot, I was keeping an eye on your kind. Go on marching, go on marching, I want you to march. We will march until we get to the riverbank because it is possible that we are going in a canoe, you doing the rowing and I striking a pose, that's the way we are going to do it. Say it: Praise Our Lord Amaro, may such a good Lord Amaro be forever praised. Now I tell myself, how can there be any other thing than my taking you to Aracaju and after that I don't know. Because if I wanted revenge there wouldn't be enough people to kill that could pay for Amaro or my sons or Luzinete's face flying toward 129 the clouds and turning into the moon and I down here with ashes on my face and crying mud, I tell you. Don't tell me anything: Our Lord Amaro be praised, may such a good Lord Amaro forever be praised, so good a Lord Amaro, go on thinking, go on thinking, and when I say his name go on thinking and crossing yourself, you have far too many sins, senhor. At first I didn't even know Amaro well, but after a while he was the best friend a man could have and he liked even frogs, he kept looking at frogs and feeling sorry for frogs and anything about frogs. There with his eyes open. That is, now that everybody is gone I am the only one left, and then. Observe those bushes with the blue glow. Would you say it was only bushes? No, you would say it was ghosts, light from dead men, bugbears smoking a pipe, but it is not that, it is a cold fire only I know, my stars. See it this way, I am in Heaven and you are in Hell, it's no use. And I don't need either to eat or to do anything else. If I feel like it I can get the Flag of the Divine Holy Ghost and hold it up and use whistles I can make from bamboos, but you don't even know what a bamboo is, and those whistles I will use to call the army of the real men, masters of this land, each one a champion and always making war, each one a saint. Then we will see who will do the talking. I used to be a sergeant, would you believe that, from the tip of my boot to the shield on my cap. Well, then I look at myself and say: You are what they call soldiers, you are a monkey, fellow. Then I am no longer a monkey. And instead of staying here to look at these refugees, these waves of people, these migrants swallowing wild beans and nothing else, and to watch the world pass, instead of that what could one have? What one could have, to prove to you that you are no good and neither is your kind, what one could have would be my army once again, for I am going to call this army once more and the whole earth

is going to see, because when I gather together that sea of

men and animals, that army, no one will ever defeat us and we will take over and I am going to make my sons on the moon.

What have I done so far? Nothing. I was not I, I was a piece of somebody else, but now I am I forever and who can stop me? I am going to take you, you pox, to the middle of Aracaju, I am going to take you to João Pessoa Street and I am going to say: If I want to be governor I am going to be governor and if you don't like it you can settle it with my army, which is almost too big for the state of Sergipe. Taking it from Canindé de São Francisco to Brejo Grande, along the river and going farther inland come the white blonds from the Command of Porto da Folha and the rough ones from Propriá, the First Regiment of the Beleathered which makes lines four hundred men long per line and there are so many lines you can't count and all ride on small horses of restless heads whose hoofs dig the ground and whose nostrils blow smoke in cold weather. These ones have spears and carry their prods under their right arms and they come down like a wind gale, a stampede over the tall grass and over whatever else is in the way, there is no force that can resist them. On each side there is a line of trumpeters blowing on steel trumpets that not even twenty of the men from here can carry and as those trumpets blow every man in their way disappears and the women who are to have children become the bearers of still things on account of those trumpets. And it is a strong race that eats couscous steeped in milk when they can, and when they can't they eat dry corn meal and they endure. They are commanded by Captain Geraldo Bonfim of the Scratchbrush, whose horse goes faster than the wind and who can gun a man down from two leagues away and who when it rains puffs the clouds away and I am the only one who can defeat him in combat, because once he beat Saint George, and he had the saint running across the prairie crying saintly cries and begging for mercy. Those have leather doublets, leggings, vests, kneepieces and footguards of reddish, dusty leather and nothing can go through that leather, whether it is a cannonpiece or whatever. Once Saint George came down to rescue a man Captain Geraldo was about to puncture because he was bad and a great bother, and he said to the captain: This man is my devotee, senhor, therefore be so kind as to let him go and on top of that say some prayers of repentance to undo your wrongdoing. At that Captain Geraldo, who had his foot on the good-for-nothing's neck, took off his hat, stroked his blond hair back, crossed himself and said to the saint: You are a good saint and deserving of respect and if this was some other time I would be most willing to acknowledge thy saintship's wish, but this man here is not worth your concern and besides he gave me the trouble of running after him on this field to rope him and please excuse me, senhor, but this living thing here is going to be bled and it is going to be now. And having said that, he made such a fearsome grimace that a tree that stood nearby wilted right away. The saint said: Well now, this is the first man who ever talked to me like that and I did not enjoy this talk, so I will lift my spear and will disembowel you, and it is going to be now. And he spurred his flying horse and pointed his spear against Captain Geraldo, but Captain Geraldo seized the spear and grinned with such glittering white teeth at the saint's horse that the horse reeled back. Oh, Saint, said Captain Geraldo, excuse me, and he hit his legging with the spear and his leggings being made of that hard leather, the spear broke into twenty-three pieces, and there was nothing the saint could do and he said only: Are you mad, man? Have you gone crazy? I wasn't before but now I am, Captain Geraldo said, and he grinned even more widely and drew out a two-meter bush knife which had so

132   much steel that two good-sized men would not be able to

carry it and said to the saint as he minced the air: You are Saint George, but may the good Lord forgive me for with this thorn of Saint Anthony I am going to do bad things if Your Saintship does not leave this state this instant. And thus seeing his horse crestfallen and his lance splintered the saint turned on his heels and threw himself through a cattle passage with Captain Geraldo right behind him and it was a chase that lasted two days and a half, over land, water, low cactus and what have you, and the captain made the ground spark with his knife which was so honed it made the air groan. Every now and then he got close to the saint but then the saint looked back, raised his head and went faster, smashing the bushes as he went and stirring up leaves and twigs everywhere, there were leaves and branches floating in the air and a noise of broken wood over the field. The saint ended up hiding behind a cloud and Captain Geraldo left him alone, went home, killed a calf and ate it and picked his teeth with the rib bones. The saint ran almost all the way from Porto da Folha to Siriri and to this day that cloud can be seen there for him to hide behind in case Captain Geraldo of the Scratchbrush should appear once again in those parts in a foul mood.

The Second Regiment of the Beleathered starts from the corner of Nossa Senhora da Glória over Carira and Frei Paulo to Socorro, and this force is commanded by Major Alligator of Carira, thus called because he has more teeth than an alligator and his mouth is bigger and he is greatly fond of laughing and they say he has neither father nor mother, having been born inside a lagoon whence he sprang up all armed, in his left hand a cross of cactus, in his right hand a silver sickle, and as soon as he emerged he beheaded those who were around the lagoon with the sickle, so as to show who was in command on this land. This regiment has several fine lieutenants, all dressed in black and white dappled 133 leather which no matter how much dust falls on it never reddens or stains. Many go to combat riding oxen and at the time of the encounter if their weapons fall they pull out the ox's horns and gore their enemies with those twisted horns, black and long. It was Major Alligator of Carira who defeated two hundred batallions of Bahians who jumped the border and the major went on defeating Bahians and defeating Bahians and the Bahians went on storming out of here and he took the opportunity to clear some land that went from Itabaiana to Poço Redondo and this will always be his farmland when the army advances and takes the lands. And these men fight shouting, so that the enemy's heart will fail just from hearing their clamor. It is like they say: Looking at the Quizongo Mountains one may see nothing, but all of a sudden the ground commences to thunder and smoke comes out from behind the mountains and that smoke starts going up, and what is it but Major Alligator of Carira who is around those parts and he bursts down the range followed by his riders and wherever he passes he uproots the trees and terrifies people. Like this: When Morcego River is full and everyone is carefree just hearing the waters flowing and smelling the scent of wet earth and expecting winged ants or something of that sort, here is Major Alligator leaping out of the river with fish jumping from his beard and when he emerges he raises such a wave that the river becomes larger than the São Francisco and then dries out from fright and all the land becomes parched, this until the major laughs and rushes headlong into the wilds, and then the river comes back little by little, until it returns with all his little fish. And when they had the war they were going to send these Major Alligator people to the war, but the Americans came and said: Don't send these Major Alligator men over here for they will leave nothing standing and then they did not send them and the war took longer.

The Third Regiment of the Beleathered starts more or less from the brinks of Simão Dias, zigzagging to Barracão and from there to Estância and Indiaroba and other places and the commander of that one is Captain Rosivaldo da Silva with Jaguar, who was brought up by some jaguars but he soon had to leave them even as a boy, because the jaguars were no match for him because when he was two months old he already raised the devil, and in fact one day when he was very upset he dug a traphole in the ground into which sank two dozen cattle herds, and this hole he dug using only his fingernails, because he did not even have any teeth yet with which to chew up the rocks that turned up, and afterward he was a cowhand for a long time. When he brought down a bull he pulled it so hard that the bull entered into the ground and several of them are still planted where he left them, such were those pulls of his and sometimes knuckle raps. When he quit he used to ride a headless mule, but it was too much work to keep it and he let it go with great sorrow, but to this day, from time to time, he goes out to the backlands and calls the mule and the two of them converse for a long time and sometimes he mounts it and spends twenty days in the wilds sightseeing with the mule and afterward he returns very contented. This regiment dresses in jaguar leather for combat, and Captain Rosivaldo wears spotted jaguar leather with the jaguar's head on top of his hat with a red blossom inside the jaguar's mouth, and he carries as a weapon a small cannon which he wears under his armpit and which is destructive to one thousand and two hundred men with each well-placed shot. There was a certain time when Captain Rosivaldo was fighting one thousand and two hundred men and no matter how much he fought he could not kill more than forty-two per minute, so all of a sudden he said: A real man will not fight in batches like this. A real man will fight in an orderly fashion. Line up over there, and I will greet you one by one. So they lined up and Captain Rosivaldo raised his cannon faster than fast and fired one single shot and not one enemy remained standing and he went back home very proudly and whistling the kind of whistle one uses to call jaguars and a great many jaguars came to celebrate. Only the jaguars complained a little of not being able to eat that whole mass of men, because those who were lying on the ground had turned into dust or else mush and many had ended up over in the state of Alagoas, such was the strength of the cannon, and they say there was a rain of ornery characters in Maranhão that day, all lined up as had been agreed.

Well then, if it comes to my mind to do it I will use my whistles and some bugles and will call this army of which I am commander and will enter Aracaju with you on parade with the ground smelling of pitanga leaves and will leave nothing in my way. They are all real men, that's what they are.

VIII 🐐

This river has little water, less water than the other rivers and much less water than the River São Francisco, but I can tell you, it's a good river. And if we are going this way it's because I got it into my mind to go this way. I think that from Santo Amaro on we can slide downriver and will soon be arriving in Barra dos Coqueiros. From there I can observe Aracaju and stay there watching and nursing my anger and there will be a fine time when I drag this over there, throw him in the middle of the street, make my delivery and wait. I delivered him, you bunch of scoundrels, I did. Now I want to see. Ahn-well, I never thought about what I am going to do afterward, for me now there is no afterward. What a shameless river, it begins to get salty from far away, it becomes like a sea, this is what angers me, because if things were right, this being called Sergipe River, it should push all this sea backward until it cried enough. But no, it goes on becoming saltier and saltier and even makes sealike waves and turns blue. I don't like all this water. What I like is sometimes to see from here the backs of the pier walls of Aracaju and those houses with big doors on the other side of Front Street and a truck here and there, sometimes a ship. If you keep on sailing, you keep on seeing the city appearing. There is a spot where you can smell the aroma of the open-air market and this island that has nothing but coconut trees. I will say that before you get to the salt water, about five or six leagues from the mouth, it's a good river. It is not a river like the São Francisco, which is a wonder, and these boats and these canoes cannot be compared with the boats and canoes from there, because a São Francisco canoe is tall and strong and hundreds of things can fit inside. In front of the city of Penedo the São Francisco may make turns but the turns are not out of weakness, they are out of capriciousness, and there is what they call the hour of the gourds, when the women go to bathe in the river and there you can fish shrimp with a piece of towline and chicken guts or whatever. You can sit on the bank with that piece of towline pulling shrimp out of the water, for they are plentiful there, and the boys catch so many shrimp that the grown-ups get tired of them. There also may be piranha, which you find in some places but not in others, with teeth that cut through steel wires and an excessive meanness. When they catch an animal that falls in the river, more than a thousand of them get together and they go squirming and going under the animal's hide which you can see bulging out and all of this makes a chirping noise, like birds. Soon there is nothing but a fleshless carcass, all clean, and the river leaves it there, just leaves it there and suddenly it becomes a piece of the river, a stone full of slime, the ground and the mud, and the piranha are never seen again until another animal goes in and they do the cleaning once more. I am not from there but I had to visit Passagem many times, but since I am not from there I don't go into the river. I get to the shallow parts wearing high boots and I put my hand under my chin and study that yellow water a long time. It's a water that doesn't even seem to be the biggest in the world as the São Francisco is, separating Sergipe from the rest above, like the Real separates the rest below, and here is all of Sergipe lying here. And after that the São Francisco goes all over Brazil and fills everything up and carries land as far as the hollow of the world, there almost cannot be anything more important. Many times, when the moon is out, the river becomes silvery, not always, but sometimes it does get silvery and you can look at it like a ribbon, glittering and glimmering. You can hear any noise that's made, like a man walking along the wet bank when it's shallow, a mooring post touching and untouching the side of a canoe or a woman talking, even far away, and we have that large quietness, sometimes one or two crickets, sometimes a lot of toads, but that's all. Now, this river here has its good things, winding across these good lands and making this confusion of water here, more or less from Maruim on. I don't even know where the bastard starts because it's likely to disappear all of a sudden and it only gathers strength around these parts, for then it goes in and out and goes out and in and it gets salty and it's something, anyone can see that.

Now, those people who live by the sea are a bad sort, they are used to having it easy. They stick a hand in the mud and pick out a mussel, a land crab, another crab, they pick up some oysters, and they eat them. What do they think about for the next day? Nothing. The sea never dries out, nor does the mud, with these swamp trees popping and making mud-flat noises that scare us as we approach and hear them. So they are always going out to the mud flats, picking up a mussel, some oysters, a land crab, and they eat them and they can go to sleep. In Aracaju, behind the Church of Saint Joseph, behind Carro Quebrado, there is a river by the name of Tamandaí, a dirty bastard, a piggish filthy bastard of a river, that when you go into it you come out with a beard of mud. Well then, crossing the sand flats and entering the swamp you find a lot of people with little poles catching crabs on the Tamandaí. And there are some tall grasses where the land is dry and there people do the worst kinds of dirty things. Seashore people are like that, they just eat and do shameless things, all of them have rows of children like an army, because everything is very easy for them. Then they become boring, talkative and fond of witnessing and testifying; they are worthless, they never have to think of the next day and that's not good. I myself don't like that kind, I find them intolerable, I become awkward and I try never to be around them, I leave them alone, I would rather stay with my own.

So they are already searching around Aracaju and I am going out at night by the river, for I know they are waiting for me in Aracaju and I don't like to have men waiting for me, it's not fitting. So. So they are waiting for me to travel to Aracaju overland. So I come by water to Barra dos Coqueiros to see how everything is and from there I cross over and take my cargo. Then they will be able to seize me. I tell you: If I want to, I can cross this shit walking. If I want to, I can drink up all this water, I dry up the river and I walk over there, only the damn water is salty and it's not easy. In Aracaju there are people who cross over every day. There is a woman called Rita the Fish who does that, to me she is crazy and so is her brother — whoever heard of people enjoying crossing such a width, swimming, every single day, I don't understand it. Well, maybe I will make you swim over, that may be, because sturdy as you are it's going to be an event, you won't get past the bank. The gums ought to be fine by now, huh? Why, such a well-done job you would never find if you paid for it. When we get there, if we get there in the early morning, we will see everything rose-colored with the sun coming up. If I want to, I can have the sun stop coming up, but I don't feel like roping the bastard today, leave it alone. Well then. If I arrive in the morning I can have all day to think and to stay there. I can anchor you in the river so that the crabs will bite your feet and you will have to dance so that the little beasts don't feast on you. But I won't do that because people would come over to see what it was all about; so that if we arrive in the early morning we camp by the bank, we cross that mud and we wait. I could get off in Aracaju with all the people waiting for me, but I won't do that. Don't think I am afraid, because fear is one thing a real man like me doesn't have, never had, never will have, and is not about to have. Fear of what? Of a couple of swollen bellies that they have over there and of some beach-side privates, all trembling because they have never seen action. I can eat them all up with a hand tied to a foot, that's why I am not afraid. But when we get there maybe there will be a very high mortality and then things will get complicated because even you can be hit in the middle of the confusion, and you are not going so easily, I tell you.

First you go to the chief's house because I want to take you and I want to look at his face and say to him: The person you sent to Paulo Afonso, I remember, right here in this room, the person you sent to Paulo Afonso one night here in this very room, I, Getúlio Santos Bezerra, having a red vermouth right here, the person you sent to Paulo Afonso to fetch this creature, was not I. Maybe he will say, what do you mean Getúlio, but didn't you get my message, what are you doing Getúlio, sit down right there and let us settle this matter, you always make me worry, Sr. Getúlio. Something like that. I say: You didn't understand what I said. I said that the man you sent to Paulo Afonso — and tell me right now did you or did you not do it? Tell me now, tell me now! I did, Sr. Getúlio, but things took another turn, let's talk. But I am telling you that the man you sent to Paulo Afonso one night right in this very room having a red vermouth, that man who left his cap hanging on the back of a chair and asked for permission to unbutton his jacket and you said yes and your son kept looking at the two bandoliers and I asked for a glass of water and he called the maid and I drank the water and it even happened then that my belly itched on the side and I kept scratching it and listening after I drank the water. That man you sent out under those conditions in the black Hudson with Amaro, who was not even there at the time and was sleeping at the station or watching the Protestants at Duque de Caxias Street because he enjoyed the singing of the Protestants, I think, well then, that man you sent out is no longer that man. I used to be him, now I am I. Hum, be a man, stand by your words because I stood by mine, take your parcel and don't turn the crank of this telephone to call anything because it's no use, for I am going to go through this door with your permission, kindly give my regards to your kin, very grateful for everything, if you need anything I am at your service although I don't know where, a great pleasure, have a good day, thank you very much, long live ourselves, if you need anything just call, now that corporal by the door, it would be better if he did not stop me, I am telling you, senhor, I am not that one you sent to Paulo Afonso anymore, I used to be him and now I am I. I will say this with my eyes on his eyes and will leave you there tied and toothless, and with my ash face and with my woman in the moon I will go out into the world. I live in the world, period. That's why I stop here and I remain waiting for the best time. Besides I want to take a good look at Aracaju. I never did get along well with Aracaju, to tell the truth. When I had nothing to do I used to take the streetcar around town and kept riding on it until I got tired of it or else I stayed at the station playing dice with whoever was around or conversing with Giba, who was one of the detectives, wore black eyeglasses

142 and hobbled a little. And that was all. Or else I went to the

chief's house and got something to eat and stayed there
mending the fence or going out for things or teaching tricks
to a large dog they had or telling stories to his son. But as
soon as I could I would go back inside Sergipe and stay there,
which I greatly preferred. I want to take a very long look at
Aracaju, nursing my anger and thinking about my life and
wondering what so many people are doing there, piled up on
those big streets. When I speak nobody there understands,
when someone speaks there I don't understand. Yes, after
this I will never set foot there again. I don't have anything.
I have my guns and my ash face and I have all this land. This
I have, this whole land I have, because I was given birth by
the land through a hole in the ground and I came out in the
middle of hot smoke and she will bear others like me, because this land is the greatest breeder in the whole world. I
mean, these people of Aracaju don't know, they will never
know, only I know what there is in this whole land and I can
run over it with the wind on my face, over water and over
land. I had no business coming here the first time, I never
had. I had my mission, this I had. And I took care of it. I had
my life, this I had too, and I lived, and if they asked me, do
you want to live a long and cowardly life or do you want to
live a short and brave life, what would I answer? I would
answer: I want to live a short, brave life, being myself and
more of myself and respected in this world and when I die
remember me like this: The Dragon is dead. He who brought
mortality to his enemies, who did not betray or yield, who
never knew his better and who bled whomever he wanted
to bleed. Now I know who I am.

That party that is coming, creature, that party that is coming across the river, you can see the rifles pointing upward
and it is plain that nobody expects to catch me easily, otherwise they wouldn't have sent out so many people. Everybody knows I am going to fight back, you hear? And there 143

are only men in uniform, look well, creature, there is not one single civilian, only the ones that receive orders, not the ones that give them. Before they finish me, creature, I am still likely to drag you seven times on this muddy beach, back and forth, and I can drag whoever is in command of this party and also as many privates as come close. I don't even want to look at faces, creature, and I don't want to talk, I think there is no need to talk now, there is the need to act. That force, that force, creature, is a weakness, and from this very place, with you tied over there to the coconut tree so that you can see a man fighting, which is something you never did in your life, trash, that force is a weakness. Come over here government weakness, I let myself loose, I let go, I go and that's the way it is, in my mind some memories, in my hand some shooting rods, and my feet standing fast, my life and the dead orange tree and the moon where Luzinete lives, take a look, creature, it's a weakness and one thousand of those men are like nothing and there are more like me here, this is a man's land, hear junk, and the land that foaled me is going to vomit me back no matter how many times I am buried, who has a friend in this world. Hey Amaro, see Amaro, look what white frogs on the floor bricks. Don't tremble, trinket, look what a land and death sliding down the river, you can't even see their faces, but see what a land this is with us planted here on the ground, aren't we the same thing? aren't we the same thing?

It's funny how those men come over and none of those men is thinking anything because all are only feeling, look well, I feel, they feel, everything feels, look at this salt water, person, which came from in there, from the wilds of Sergipe, and arrives slowly, the rivers, Morcego, Cotinguiba, Jacarecica, Ganhamoroba, Poxi, Pomonga and the Vaza-Barril and the Piauí and the Itamerim and the Siriri and the Japaratuba, see, creature, it's even beautiful this water com-

ing out from back there, isn't all this one single thing? my
ash face, my hair of earth, my leather boot, my iron gun, huh
creature? aren't we all the same? not much so now because
I am I, Getúlio Santos Bezerra and my name is a verse which
is always going to be versed and if there is a moon out it
glows and if the sun is out it burns the face and if it's cold
it takes the warmth away, ay two clay bulls and a matchbox
and a pannier full of clay, I sing out a cattle chant you sing
out a cattle chant, huh Amaro, hey-hey, we are sailors and
we fly the big sail and we pull up our anchor, oy-laray, we
fly the big sail, see there Amaro, I am bigger than the king
of Hungary, on the second of February there is a festival in
Capela, huh thing, you know where Capela is? you know
where Capela is, you know where Capela is, and where is
Capela? and where is Salgado and where is Lagarto? and
where are we? hey, here they come, watch, and so slowly one
doesn't even feel, back home all have wives and couscous
and a litter, see this well, more people are born each day in
this land, it is like a storm of people showing up in this world
of my God, whatever for, huh? and I being I, being I, when
I was a boy I ate clay and entered the ground eating clay,
shitting clay and eating again, hey creature, look at life, there
comes the force, in Japaratuba there is sugar cane and the
sugar cane field is blond, blond like people from Porto da
Folha and people who are born in Muribeca are Muribecians
or Muribecards, huh Amaro? when I entered Luzinete, I entered and I stayed, my saintly little saint on the moon, my
saintly little saint and the banana bombs you threw on the
men, why don't we laugh a little, creature? what are you
seeing there, creature, the ground? this is all one big greenness when it rains and when it doesn't rain it is a yellowness,
but you can throw yourself down on the ground because
there is no danger, it will embrace you, maybe even eat you
and you turn into a tree or you turn into a land crab or your 145

excellency can turn into a stone, and even if it's hot and the rain smokes, even so, it will embrace you, believe me, and you can stay there, because that's where one has to stay anyhow, one has to stay in the ground, have you once upon a time cried, creature? not from the outside to the inside, but from the inside to the outside, yanking and digging inside? I have not done it myself, but maybe I will cry now, because I feel like crying a little now, you thing, you junk, you trash, maybe I will cry now, since it's not that I am afraid, I am not afraid even of ghosts, but I can cry because I never spoke with that weakness force nor am I ever going to and there are so many things I could not do because I did not know and the whole world stopped here, huh Amaro? see this water and this riverbank, with this light noise night and day, see this water and Aracaju and the Emperor's Bridge, see these people crossing over on boats after us and carrying guns pointing upward and that ship stopped there, it does not even know what is taking place, there are some men there playing dominoes and thinking about life, but however fate is making turns, huh Amaro? over on the moon, and believe me I am alive in Hell, over on the moon is Luzinete and if this force can shoot I can shoot too, oh my shotgun, oh my rifle and a cactus with its head up I am going to die and never going to die I am never going to die Amaro I am never going to die a cattle chant and a life Amaro aaaaaaaaaaaaaaaaahhh eeeeeeeeeeeeeeeh a-ay a-ay a-ay a-ay a-ay a-ay a-ay a-ay a-ay a-ay yeh-oh yeh-oh a-ay a-ay a-ay a-ay a-ay I am never going to die Amaro and Luzi neteonthe moon these bullets are like my finger far away and lookthere Ara I seecaju and the waterrun ningslow ly and saltyit isgood I am ne vergoingto diene verIamI, ay a clay bull, ayaclay aya-claybull claya-ay a-ay a-ay ayapan nierfull of clay and lifeI am I and will and who was ay mywiltedo rangetree ay hey I will and carry out and do and